DEFIANT T

Nic

A World War 3 Technothriller Action Event

Copyright © 2022 Nicholas Ryan

The right of Nicholas Ryan to be identified as the author of this work has been asserted by him in accordance with the copyright, Designs and Patents Act 1988.

This is a work of fiction. Names, characters, places, and incidents either are the product of the author's imagination or are used fictitiously. Any resemblance to actual persons, living or dead, events, or locales is entirely coincidental.

All rights reserved. No part of this publication may be reproduced, stored in or introduced into a retrieval system, or transmitted, in any form, or by any other means (electronic, mechanical, photocopying, recording or otherwise) without the prior written permission of the author. Any person who does any unauthorized act in relation to this publication may be liable to criminal prosecution and civil claims for damages.

Dedication:
For Ebony; the girl of my dreams.
-Nick.

About the Series:

The WW3 novels are a chillingly authentic collection of action-packed combat thrillers that envision a modern war where the world's superpowers battle on land, air and sea using today's military hardware.

Each title is a 50,000-word stand-alone adventure that forms part of an ever-expanding series, with several new titles published every year.

Facebook: https://www.facebook.com/NickRyanWW3
Website: https://www.worldwar3timeline.com
Cover design by: Other Worlds Design

Links to other titles in the collection:
- Charge to Battle
- Enemy in Sight
- Viper Mission
- Fort Suicide
- The Killing Ground
- Search and Destroy
- Airborne Assault
- Defiant to the Death
- A Time for Heroes

The Korean Peninsula in Conflict

The outskirts of Seoul had been turned into a wretched gruesome wasteland; a stinking blood-drenched morass littered with the burned-out ruins of thousands of armored vehicles.

The North Korean invasion force that had swept across the DMZ beneath a curtain of savage artillery fire had reached the gates of the capital and there been beaten back by desperate Allied defiance. In the wake of the fighting, tens of thousands were dead, their bodies heaped into ghastly piles on street corners awaiting the bulldozers that would sweep them into massed graves. Many of the corpses were so bloated and riven with bullet wounds that they were barely recognizable. The remains swelled in the heat, turning purple beneath swarms of flies. The stench of death and decomposition hung over the smoldering ruins of the city like a putrid cloud.

Out of the carnage the Allies counter-attacked.

Now the battle for Seoul was over and the North Koreans were falling back – not in a panicked retreat but in a fighting withdrawal, grimly contesting every inch of ground they had won during their initial onslaught.

Into that cauldron of flames and fury advanced the American and South Korean forces, driving headlong through a hail of enemy fire and a storm of roaring artillery.

Each yard had to be fought for and paid with blood. Every rise of ground had to be contested, every small village bought back with the bodies of the brave.

In the days after the North Korean drive towards Seoul had been stalled, it was Allied air superiority that had turned the tide of the war. But as the North Koreans withdrew across the DMZ, more and more advanced Chinese fighter jets joined the conflict, flying from military bases around Pyongyang to blunt the Allied air attacks. Heavy rain swept over the Peninsula and the fighting on the ground turned into a war of attrition.

The Allied technological edge was nullified by the sheer weight of North Korean numbers and the fanatical, suicidal sacrifice of their soldiers. Time and time again they counter-attacked in endless waves, throwing themselves onto the Allied guns until the fields and highways and hills were thick with the dead.

Allied Command sensed the enemy were on the brink of collapse. They pushed more men forward, pressing the North Koreans along the entire length of the battlefront until the relentless strain inevitably took its toll. Northwest of Seoul, in the farm fields around the tiny village of Daeseongdong-gil, the enemy's perimeter finally collapsed, and the Allies poured through.

In an instant, the measured withdrawal of the North Korean Army turned into a panic-stricken rout. The Allies rushed tanks and APCs forward while the North Koreans and their Chinese Allies scrambled to staunch the breakthrough. The enemy troops fell back into prepared defensive positions as the Americans poised themselves for the telling blow that would fracture the line apart and hurl the enemy back in disarray.

Suddenly the fighting on the Korean Peninsula centered on a single city upon whose capture would hinge the outcome of the entire war.

Kaesong.

PAJU-SI
GYEONGGI PROVINCE, SOUTH KOREA
30 KLM NORTHWEST OF SEOUL

Chapter 1:

Lieutenant Colonel Benedict Gallman shrugged off his heavy jacket and hung it over the back of his chair, then impulsively reached for the glass case on his desk as if to reassure himself it was still there; still safe.

It was.

He stared at the helmet contained within the display cabinet. His eyes drifted over the three raised silver stars and then scanned the scratched green paint, noting each nick and scar as if, by the sheer force of his gaze, he could compel the object to reveal its secrets.

His lips moving, he read the inscription carved into the brass plaque again. "Bastogne, December 1944."

He had been at Brigade headquarters for the entire morning and had returned wrung out and buzzing from too much coffee. Now he steeled himself for the task ahead. He dropped into his chair, then thrust out his chin.

"Send him in!" His eyes flicked once more to General George S. Patton's helmet as if to draw strength from the great man who had worn it.

"Sir!" The voice on the opposite side of the desk startled Gallman and he jerked his eyes up with a stab of guilt.

"Hector," he said the name contemptuously and peered at the man before him. Captain John Hector was standing stiffly to attention, staring blank-faced and expressionless over Gallman's head, his gaze fixed on a mark on the opposite wall of the bunker. The seconds of tense silence drew out and Gallman let them. He was in no hurry; a silent display of power and authority.

Finally, Captain Hector lowered his eyes.

"Stand at ease, Captain," Gallman picked up a sheaf of papers from his desk and rifled through them, his face darkening as he flicked through each one. He threw them back down on the desk, stirring up a small cloud of dust.

"You can't be surprised I summoned you."

"No, sir."

"Do you have an explanation for the events of last night and the early hours of this morning?"

"A misunderstanding, sir."

Gallman blinked, then gaped, and in the stunned seconds of silence the outrage came upon him, darkening his face until it seemed to swell with fury and scorn.

"A fucking *misunderstanding?*" he shouted the words and snatched at the file of paperwork again, tearing at the pages and holding each one up in turn. "Four of your soldiers are being held by MPs on every charge in the damn book. Three more are in hospital! There is an Australian S.A.S operator with a fractured jaw and over a dozen other men with minor injuries! You call that a misunderstanding?"

"The fight was a mistake," John Hector stared down at the Lieutenant Colonel. He could see the top of the other man's head and noticed how his thinning hair had been vainly swept across the scalp to disguise the onset of premature baldness.

"What was the fight about?"

"I'd rather not say, sir."

"I don't give a rat's ass what you'd prefer, Captain. What was the god-damned fight about?" Gallman's gaze turned pale and cold. His eyes were set close together and his large rubbery lips seemed to keep moving long after he finished speaking. Hector smiled secretly and it brought a crimson flush onto the Lieutenant Colonel's cheeks. "Well?"

Hector sighed and feigned a grimace. "The Australians said our Lieutenant Colonel was a piss-poor example of an officer. They said you spent all your time sitting on your ass miles behind the front and that you were afraid to show your face where the bullets were flying. Naturally, the fight broke out because my men were defending your reputation, sir," Hector inflected the honorific in a way that made it sound like an insult.

It was a lie, of course. The fight had been about NFL players and the obscene amounts of money they were being paid to play football.

Slowly the expression on Gallman's face changed. The blood drained from his cheeks and his eyes became hard little stones. His mouth pinched into a tight pale line and when he spoke his voice was a terrible croak of barely-suppressed fury.

"You're a smart-ass, Hector, and your company of culprits is the worst, least disciplined unit in the Battalion. You're lucky the Brigade Commander doesn't fire you and your entire damn command team – and he would if we didn't need your asses right now."

Hector said nothing. Gallman pounced from his chair, his fists opening and clenching by his side. He stomped to the far side of the bunker, ducking his head below the ceiling of logs and earth that protected the command post from enemy artillery fire. It took a long time for the Lieutenant Colonel to compose himself. Hector stood, relaxed and expressionless, while the other man prowled the revetted sandbag walls like a caged lion. Finally, Gallman stopped and turned, and there was a malicious, vengeful smile on his face.

"Your men want to fight?" Gallman's voice turned dark and menacing. "Good. You're going to get all the opportunities you can handle. 'C' Company is being moved back up to the battlefront. You'll be temporarily relieving troops from 'A' Company, 2nd Battalion, 168th Infantry Regiment who have been on the frontline since the Battle of Seoul. They're dug in ten miles northwest of here at a place called Daeseongdong-gil. HQ is gathering troops for a push north towards Kaesong tomorrow. Your men will be part of that attack. Understand?"

"Yes, sir," Hector said without emotion.

"Make your preparations, inform your men, and report back here at 1800 for final instructions. You're dismissed, Captain."

*

There were ten soldiers assembled in the mud around John Hector's Oshkosh M-ATV command vehicle: his Executive Officer, the First Sergeant, two Platoon leaders, four Platoon Sergeants, the FIST Lieutenant and her FIST Sergeant. Hector made eye contact with each person to acknowledge them and then snatched the cigarette from the corner of his mouth to issue his Warno (Warning Order).

Traditionally the Warno included an outline of the situation, the mission, the manner of execution, service and support. It was used to give subordinates advance notice of an upcoming operation to allow them time to make preparations. John Hector's Warno had a lot of blank spaces. He told them the little information he knew, and where they were destined. The Company had come off the front lines just five days ago. Now they were going back to war and the mood amongst the assembled group was one of grumbling resentment.

"We're getting this shit-show mission because the Lieutenant Colonel has a grudge against 'Culprit' Company," the First Sergeant gave his unfiltered cynical opinion.

Traditionally 'C' Company in a Battalion was known as 'Charlie' Company, but John Hector's group of misfits and trouble-makers had received so many warnings for ill-discipline and so many official rebukes for insubordination that the rest of the Battalion had shunned the unit and renamed it 'Culprit' Company.

"No. This is because he's pissed that half the god-damned men got involved in a massive brawl last night," Hector corrected, and then went on quickly, talking over the top of the inevitable chorus of protested innocence. "When is our new Lieutenant due?"

First Sergeant Ethan Breevor glanced at his watch. He was the highest ranking senior enlisted soldier in the Company and the most combat-experienced man in the unit. He was a squat, square-shouldered man with a barrel chest and the scarred, gnarled appearance of an old mountain bobcat. "Any time now," he said, and turned to stare into the middle distance where troops were milling about in the black glutinous mud as though he expected to see the replacement officer emerge out of the chaos. A truck roared past in low gear, spraying grime and belching diesel fumes.

"What do we know about him?"

Breevor shrugged. "I don't even know his name. He's a rookie, fresh out of IOBC (Infantry Officer Basic Course)."

"A rookie? Jesus H. Christ. This ain't the place for some FNG (fucking new guy) to learn his trade," Hector groaned in exasperation, then, with a shrug of fatalistic acceptance and a bitter sigh, he set the subject aside and moved on. "Okay. Tell me what we'll need for this mission that we don't already have?"

"We need our men out of the brig," the Lieutenant of 1st Platoon said.

"We need to know if the men in hospital can be discharged, otherwise we're going to the front undermanned," the XO frowned, already wrestling with the logistics of the move order.

"We need some kit," Ethan Breevor said.

Hector nodded. It was a place to start. "Okay, Sergeant, get the men on it. Find whatever gear you need and beg, borrow, or steal." He turned to his XO. "Gayle, we're going to have to sweet-talk the MPs and menace the medics. That's your job. I want every one of our guys not on a serious charge and not in a plaster cast on the trucks when we pull out tonight, understand?"

Lieutenant Gayle Nordenman nodded.

"I have a final briefing with Gallman at 1800," Hector went on, addressing his Platoon leaders. "We'll be moving out sometime after that. Inform your men and get them busy. I want ammo checks, equipment checks… and I want packs checked, gentlemen," he stared hard into the eyes of his Lieutenants. "If you find someone's carrying booze, I want it emptied into the mud before we leave. Am I clear?"

It wouldn't be the first time a soldier tried to smuggle hard liquor into a combat zone to take the edge off his frayed nerves.

*

Hector noticed a knot of the Battalion's officers standing in a huddle outside a camouflaged mess tent, their heads close together in desultory conversation. He sloshed through the sucking mud, and the group's ranks opened for him grudgingly.

The Captain of Bravo Company, a dour-faced toad of a man, regarded Hector with the same expression he might consider something disgusting he had stepped in.

"Word around the camp is that your band of trouble-makers are moving up to the battlefront," the officer sneered. "Good riddance."

"Makaby, you really are a prize turd," John Hector said with a taunting lazy smile. His eyes were as cold and glittering as the steel edge of a dagger. "And if I get the chance, I'm going to kick your head in before this war's over…" the smile stayed fixed on Hector's lips, his tone never changing from conversational banter. But the implicit promise of violence behind his affable voice was unmistakable.

Another officer thrust a mug of coffee into Hector's hands and the bristling tension between the two Captains diffused, washed away by other voices.

"Intel is saying the North Koreans have fallen back to a series of prepared emplacements, and it's going to be a bitch to winkle them out."

"I overheard Gallman tell the Supply Sergeant the entire Battalion is on the move," a tall cadaverous Lieutenant revealed.

"S2 said the Chinese are pouring south to reinforce the bastards…"

A truck stopped on the far side of the tent and a young officer in a clean uniform swung out through the passenger door and jumped down into the ankle-deep mud with a ruck on his shoulder. He gave the driver a wave and the truck bellowed away into the distance, its chunky tires churning for traction.

The young man turned with a bewildered expression on his face. Hector made the connection instinctively.

"Aw, shit." He tossed the dregs of his coffee into the mud and strode towards the officer.

"You're looking for me," he said as he drew closer. "I'm Captain John Hector, Commander of 'C' Company, 9th Battalion, 33rd Infantry regiment, 19th Infantry Division," he explained. "And you're my new Lieutenant."

"Sir, yes, sir!" the young officer stiffened and snapped a parade ground salute. His eyes were red-raw, his face drawn and pale – and he looked impossibly young. "Second Lieutenant Richard Curry, reporting for duty, sir."

"Curry?" Hector looked bored. He gave the Lieutenant a once-over, decided he would be lucky to survive twenty-four hours in combat, then shrugged.

"You'll be leading 2nd Platoon," Hector pointed to a shanty town of filthy mud-spattered tents that denoted the bivouac. "Their Lieutenant was killed five days ago on the outskirts of Seoul. They're good men."

Lieutenant Curry looked overwhelmed by the grime and the slum-like conditions of an army in camp. Trucks and APCs were parked on the verge of rutted tracks and the earth-churned fields were filled with hundreds of men. The sound was like the noise of a far-off ocean; the tumult of countless voices over the constant throaty rumble of vehicle engines. It was a far cry from the neat barracks and parade grounds of Officer's School at Fort Benning.

"But before you meet your guys," Hector fixed the rookie Second Lieutenant with a sudden piercing glare, "I just want to be sure you understand your priorities. So, tell me, what's your first objective?"

Curry reacted like an automaton; repeating lines that had been drilled into him. "To gain the confidence of the men I will be commanding, sir."

"No."

"No, sir?"

"No," Hector said. "Your first objective is to realize you are an idiot and you don't command shit. You lead. Second, you know nothing about combat, and nothing about leadership. You're dangerous to everyone around you. So do as your Sergeant tells you, and you might just stay alive. That's an order."

*

"The North Koreans aren't going to give up without a hell of a fight," Lieutenant Colonel Gallman began the 1800 briefing, keeping his tone crisp and business-like, his disdain for John Hector hidden behind an expressionless mask. "They're fanatics, they're absolutely devoted to their Dear Leader, and they regard being repulsed from Seoul as a humiliating loss of face. At the moment they're reinforcing the area around Kaesong, north of the DMZ, and digging in for a fight to the death."

John Hector shuffled a little closer to a map pinned on the wall and studied it carefully. Gallman used the tip of his finger to point out the critical terrain.

"Kaesong is our ultimate objective. The area is broken into two distinct parts; the Kaesong Industrial Region to the south, and the city of Kaesong itself a few clicks further north. But before we can attack the city, we have to secure a route through this broad valley, bordered by two pieces of high ground. To the west is Hill 547 and to the east is Hill 581," he circled the two prominent features. "They're about three clicks apart, and both of them overlook the route to Kaesong."

"It's a death trap," Hector gave his bleak opinion.

"It's a strong defensive position," was as much as Gallman would concede. "Intel says the North Koreans have been preparing this location for months – since before the war started. They've dug a maze of deep trench positions, and they've created a series of fixed concrete emplacements."

"Emplacements?" Hector frowned.

"Bunkers," Gallman said. "Some are dug in tanks they've turned into pill-boxes; some are anti-tank emplacements. We don't know exactly how many there are, or where they are all sited because the North Koreans learned the art of *maskirovka* from the Russians – and the Ruskies are the god-damned world champions at this kind of shit."

Maskirovka was a military doctrine employed by the Russians dating back to the early twentieth century that outlined a range of measures used for military deception, including camouflage, decoys, and misdirection. The doctrine had played a key part in Russian victories at Stalingrad and the Battle of Kursk during the Second World War.

"All we do know from satellite imagery is that the valley is well defended by camouflaged fixed emplacements and reinforced bunkers, most probably connected to their infantry trenches through a maze of rebarred concrete transit tunnels. Several of these emplacements have been identified and will be targeted by artillery before the attack goes in… but Intel doesn't know if the bunkers they've located are real, or if they're the decoys."

"Jesus…" Hector breathed.

"The North Koreans will have artillery observers on the hills and probably anti-aircraft SAM sites bristling with 9K35 Strela-10 short-range surface-to-air missile systems. The SAMs are not your concern, obviously, but their positioning is going to make air support for the attack problematic. I wouldn't be counting on our heroic Air Force brothers to risk their expensive fighter-bombers if shit gets real."

Hector grunted. Rivalry between the Army and the Air Force wasn't anything new. Most soldiers had nothing but contempt for Air Force personnel who they believed fought the war from a distance and from comfortable air-base accommodation, while the blood-and-guts work was left to the grunts on the ground.

"And behind all that hardware and manpower is still the enemy's artillery," Gallman came to the end of his tactical analysis with a final grim warning. "We've taken a lot of their heavy long-range pieces out with air and missile attacks, but not all of it. You can be sure the NKs have plenty of short and medium range stuff that they can still throw at us."

Gallman pinned a second map to the wall. It showed the North Korean side of the DMZ. He handed Hector a couple of satellite images and a black and white photograph of a trench line. "Your Company will move out at 2100 tonight. Your destination is here," he pointed to a location on the photograph. "This is the North Korean bunker system they had in place to defend their side of the DMZ. When they fell back, we occupied their trenches. That is where your men will spend the night. A staff liaison officer from the 168th will meet you and guide you forward to your positions. It will be your jumping off point tomorrow morning."

Hector studied the photo and satellite images carefully. The abandoned trenches stood directly in line with the valley they had to charge through. "We're going to be in the center of the attack?"

"You'll be supported on both flanks by troops from the 168th, and mechanized infantry in Brads," Gallman said airily, ducking the question. "The attack calls for three full Battalions of light and mechanized infantry supported by Abrams tanks and artillery."

Hector looked bleak. If the artillery and Air Force didn't hammer the waiting North Koreans to a bloody pulp, this would be a suicide mission.

He imagined his men bursting over the lip of the trench and running onto the enemy's machine guns, floundering through the mud and grime and choking smoke while the North Korean artillery and mortars picked them to pieces at will. He had the sudden unbidden recollection of an appalling photograph he had seen of the Great War in Belgium;

thousands of First World War infantrymen swarming across the hell of a barbed-wire strewn no-man's land while German machine gunners slaughtered the charging soldiers in their droves.

He cringed, and tiny insects of fear crawled across his arms and plucked at the strings of his nerves. A century of warfare and technological advances had passed since WWI, and yet very little had changed for the beleaguered infantryman.

"Is there anything else, sir?" Hector shook off the nightmare images, suddenly somber and quietly dismayed.

"No. That's it. The attack goes in at dawn tomorrow morning." Gallman saw the blanched look on Hector's face and the corner of his mouth tugged into a secret cruel smile. It gave him a great deal of satisfaction to see the big arrogant bastard subdued.

Hector stepped out of the gloom of the command bunker and into the light of the setting sun. The clouds overhead had thinned to reveal a sky tinged with golden and crimson hues. He took a deep breath to appreciate the moment, like it might be the last sunset he ever saw. Then he sloshed through the mire to his command vehicle and leaned in through the passenger-side door.

"Guidons, guidons, guidons," he snatched for the radio mic mounted to the IAN/PRC-117G multiband radio on the Oshkosh's dashboard. "This is Culprit Six, my location in twenty for a Mike Whisky update. Acknowledge."

*

At 2100 hours 'Culprit' Company clambered aboard a fleet of Oshkosh M-ATVs and two M1083 canvas-covered trucks for the journey to the battlefront.

The four vehicles transporting 1st Platoon were in the vanguard, followed by the headquarters element which included Hector's command M-ATV, the two M1083s carrying the Supply Sergeant and the XO, followed by two more M-ATVs transporting First Sergeant Ethan Breevor and the unit's medics. At the tail of the command element were a final two M-ATVs for the FIST team and the mortar team.

Close behind the command element vehicles were the M-ATVs of 2nd and 3rd Platoons, so the column stretched like an unwieldy snake across the landscape, bunching close together through the corners and uncoiling along the stretches of straight highway that lead north.

The roads were pock-marked with artillery craters; the devastated and ruined landscape concealed by the shroud of darkness. Leaning forward in the passenger seat of his command vehicle, Hector kept peering through the windshield, all his attention focused on the horizon. The skyline flickered and winked angry red, and beneath the rumble of revving engines the muted but persistent thunder of artillery fire seemed unending.

In 2nd Platoon's lead vehicle, Lieutenant Curry sat, swaying from side to side, as the vehicle jounced and jolted along the debris-littered road. His head was down, and in his hands was a pocket-sized Bible. His mouth moved silently over the words as he flicked through several dog-eared pages.

"Are you praying, Lieutenant?" A villainous-looking Corporal sat opposite the Lieutenant with a bemused look on his ugly face. A pale puckered scar ran down the soldier's cheek and when he smiled mockingly, Curry saw the man's front two teeth were missing. The creases of the Corporal's weather-beaten face were crusted with ingrained grime and his voice was a guttural rasp.

Curry gave the Corporal an avuncular smile. "Just reading."

"Are you calling to God?"

"God is around us all the time. He's here with us right now."

"No," the Corporal shook his head and there was something terrible and haunted in the man's eyes that sent a chill down the rookie Lieutenant's spine. "God's not here, Lieutenant. This right here is Hell."

Curry closed the Bible and slipped it back into his breast pocket. He looked deeply troubled for a moment. "Where else would God be right now, at a time like this?"

The Holy Spirit's whereabouts remained undecided because the night suddenly lit up with a wicked searing flash of fire and the M-ATV they were traveling in lurched off the road and ran headlong into a drainage ditch. The roar of the explosion was deafening. A sound like hammering hail clattered against the steel side of the vehicle.

The men piled out of the M-ATV, bruised and battered by the bone-jarring collision. Richard Curry scraped the back of his hand across his brow and looked astonished when it came away smeared with blood. Another enemy artillery round came shrieking and howling out of the night sky.

"Get into cover!"

The entire convoy came to a skidding halt. The soldiers scrambled from their vehicles and ran for the shelter of a slime-filled roadside ditch. They threw themselves down in the glutinous mud just as the second artillery round exploded fifty yards away on the far side of the road. The earth heaved up and the ground around the soldiers trembled. Shrapnel fragments fizzed through the air and peppered the exposed hulls of the M-ATVs.

"Anyone hurt? Anyone injured?" John Hector came sprinting down the verge of the road, agitated and wild eyed. "Buff? Any casualties?"

The villainous Corporal shook his head. "The new Lieutenant's got a bump. Everyone else is okay."

The rising crescendo of a third incoming artillery round howled in Hector's ears and he threw himself sideways, into the muddy ditch. The sound of it was a shrieking scream as it plunged down out of the darkness and exploded, destroying one of 3rd Platoon's M-ATVs near the tail of the column. The vehicle was heaved into the air by the impact and torn apart. Fragments of white-hot metal went cartwheeling into the sky and fell back to earth in twisted, smoldering chunks.

"Buff, take a couple of men and check it out. Make sure the guys in Three Platoon are okay," Hector ordered the Corporal.

The big soldier dragged himself out of the mire and went away into the night in a running crouch, shadowed by two other men. Hector glanced at Richard Curry. The Lieutenant's face was pale, and under the hand he had pressed to his forehead was a lump the size of a golf ball and an inch-long cut.

"Have a medic check you out when the shelling stops," Hector took a dismissive glance at the injury.

"Yes, sir," Curry said and then after a pause asked meekly. "Is Buff a good man?"

"Buff?"

"The Corporal."

Hector smiled wryly. "His name is Loftham, and yes, he's a good man... so long as you don't call him Buff."

"It's some kind of nickname?"

"Yeah," Hector said. Around him men were slowly rising from the drainage ditch and checking their equipment, sensing that, for the moment at least, the artillery barrage had ended. "It's short for Big Ugly Fat Fucker... but I wouldn't recommend you try it out. He's likely to rip your head off your shoulders and shit down your neck."

The Corporal came back, sauntering, the tension gone from his body as he too sensed the shelling had ceased. "The vehicle was the only casualty," he reported to Hector. "She's been blown to bits. All the men are okay."

Hector dragged himself from the ditch and stood with his hands on his hips, surveying the damage. A pair of slitted, dipping headlights appeared from out of the north, coming closer, the vehicle's engine howling in high gear. It was a Humvee. It braked to a halt at the head of the column and a Sergeant came striding down the road, M4 in his hands.

"You're in command?"

"Yeah," Hector met the Sergeant. "What the fuck just happened?"

"The 'crazies' have infiltrated artillery OPs behind our lines," the Sergeant growled. The North Koreans had colloquially been labeled 'crazies' by the Americans because of their fanatical, suicidal attacks. "Every time a column moves north, they call in fire."

"They must be close by."

"Yeah."

On an impulse, Hector sent First Platoon one click west into the darkness and Third Platoon one click east. The infantry scoured the unfamiliar crater-torn terrain and were about to call off their search when a startled soldier stumbled into a grave-sized hole and fell on top of two North Korean artillery observers. A panicked shout of shock ripped through the night and then a flurry of automatic fire, the muzzle flash bright as a torch in the darkness. When First Platoon returned to the roadside, they were dragging the two dead North Korean corpses behind them, the enemy soldiers' bodies bullet-riddled and gruesomely disfigured.

'Culprit' Company remounted their vehicles and pushed cautiously on into the night. After fifteen tense minutes they drove up to a pontoon bridge. Hector pulled his command vehicle to the side of the road and waited until the entire column had made the transit safely. On the banks of the river, he could see the twisted ruins of three other destroyed pontoon bridges and the burned out remains of several Abrams tanks and Strykers. There were dark body-sized lumps scattered along the riverbank and the night was alive with the scurry of rats, feeding on the rotting remains of the dead. The river was oily black and the water stank of something rotting and putrid.

Hector re-mounted his vehicle and drove across the bridge – into North Korea.

Chapter 2:

The roadside sign ghosted out of the dark night. It was a wooden post with pieces of crate nailed haphazardly to it, indicating approximate distances to New York, Los Angeles and several other American cities. Across the top of the sign, hand painted in crude black lettering, was the legend, *'Welcome to the Apocalypse'*. Below the lettering someone with a dark sense of humor had graffitied, *'Please wipe your feet before entering.'*

The convoy of vehicles rolled down a gentle slope and came to a stop in the lee of a high earthen rampart. Hector climbed down from his Oshkosh and stood like a lost tourist in a foreign city for a moment.

The administrative area of the 2nd Battalion, 168th Infantry Regiment was in a small gully bordered by a ragged line of high man-made earthen ramparts. The Command Post was a tent, surrounded by freshly-dug slit trenches, that stood astride a well-worn muddy path leading to the crest of the rise.

An officer poked his head out through the entrance to the tent. He looked hard at Hector and narrowed his eyes suspiciously.

"Are you Hector from 'Charlie' Company, 9th Battalion, 33rd?"

"Yes," Hector answered.

The officer came from the tent and straightened, his hand outthrust. "I'm Major Gill, Battalion Executive Officer. Good to have you here."

The two men shook hands. Gill was a thin, wiry man with a squint and a sparse covering of dark hair. He ran his eye over the mud-spattered convoy of parked vehicles and then returned his attention to Hector. "Lieutenant Colonel Wise is at a Regimental briefing in preparation for tomorrow's attack. He'll catch up with you when he returns. In the meantime, I'm sure your men are tired and hungry. I'll have a staff officer take you up to the trench line and show you your billet for the night."

A sudden rain squall swept over the valley, soaking the men, and Major Gill looked skyward with irritation. "If this damned rain doesn't let up, we'll need boats tomorrow morning…"

"Is there an option for postponing the attack?" Hector asked.

"No. It's out of the question. We've got the North Koreans on the back foot and every extra day of respite allows them to fortify their position further. The attack goes ahead, rain, hail or shine… Waterson!"

A nervous-looking Lieutenant appeared from inside the command tent in answer to the Major's bellowed summons. "Take Captain Hector and his Platoon leaders up into the trenches and introduce them to the Captain of 'Alpha' Company."

"Yes, sir."

Gill and Hector shook hands a final time. Gill offered a last piece of advice. "You might want to turn your Company over to your Executive Officer. He can get your men fed while you're making your inspection and arranging the relief-in-place."

Hector nodded, then sent for his Platoon leaders. Gayle Nordenman arrived with them.

"You're waiting here for a while, Gayle," Hector explained. "Have the men chow down, and start unloading all the gear from the vehicles."

Lieutenant Waterson led the way into the night, negotiating a narrow causeway between slit trenches and then climbing the rise towards the crest of the rampart. The mud was ankle-deep and a rope tether line had been strung as a hand-hold. The column of figures trekked up the incline like a rope-team of mountain climbers scaling Everest; leaning far forward to maintain their balance against the steep gradient.

When they reached the thirty-foot high summit, Hector was breathing hard, sweating under the material of his uniform despite the misting rain. Lieutenant Waterson paused and turned in a slow circle.

"These are the positions the North Koreans built to defend their border of the DMZ," he explained. "This network of trenches stretches right across the country in some form or another. Here, north of Seoul, they're an extensive and sophisticated system of tunnels, emplacements and revetments we still haven't had time to fully explore."

Hector peered back into the night gloom and couldn't help but feel a sense of astonished awe. A few days ago, these trenches had been overrun by American and South Korean infantry. He found it difficult to comprehend as he tried to visualize Allied soldiers heroically clambering up the escarpment and charging into the hail of North Korean machine gun fire; the appalling casualties, the smoke, the explosions and the terror.

Waterson led them down a series of steps that had been cut into the compacted earth, and suddenly they were standing in ten-foot-deep sandbag-revetted trenches that zig-zagged away into the darkness. Here and there amidst the mud and the filth they saw small flickers of hooded light; men sitting on fire steps to smoke cigarettes, or navigating their way through the trench maze with flashlights. Dark critter-like shapes scurried and scampered in the shadows.

The fetid mingled odors of muddy earth, overlaid with the nauseating reek of rotting bodies, raw sewage and the smell of sweat was overpowering. Hector heard Lieutenant Curry gag and dry retch. The stench coated the back of their throats, oily and stomach-turning.

They trudged along a platform of wooden duck-boards to a bunker that had been hewn into the living rock and reinforced with a ceiling of cross-hatched logs and concrete. Across the opening was a tattered scrap of grimy canvas that screened the interior. Waterson twitched it aside and they stepped into a large underground area cluttered with crude furnishings and radio equipment, lit with pale watery lamp-light.

The commander of Alpha Company, 2nd Battalion, 168th Infantry Regiment was a haggard-faced Captain with bloodshot eyes and a scruffy three-day beard. His uniform was spattered with filth and he smelled of unwashed sweat. He looked up when the group entered the bunker. His eyes were haunted, set deep in their sunken sockets.

"Hector?"

"Yeah."

The Captain nodded. He stood leaning over a table strewn with maps. Hector stepped closer and when the Captain pointed to a position on the map Hector noticed the other man's left hand was wrapped in a blood-soaked bandage.

"This is our position," the Captain said without preamble. "We're covering this half mile-long stretch of trenches. I've got 1st Platoon to the left, 2nd Platoon to the right and 3rd Platoon in the center, where we are right now. I can call my Platoon leaders in if your men want to talk to them, but frankly you're not going to be here long enough to learn anything useful. The attack kicks off at dawn tomorrow and – if you want my opinion, it's a fucking suicide mission."

"What do you know about the North Korean positions?"

"They've been shelling us consistently for the past three days," the Captain said and then flinched as the sound of an artillery round exploded somewhere west of the bunker. It had landed a long way off, but still the man twitched. He looked to Hector like he was clinging desperately to the frayed strands of his nerves, worn down by the relentless, incessant fear and danger.

"Where exactly are the North Koreans?"

"Here," the Captain drew a line between the two hills Hector had seen on Benedict Gallman's map. "You know that quote from the Bible – something about walking through the valley of the shadow of death?"

Hector nodded slowly.

"Well, I reckon that's what is waiting for you at dawn tomorrow," he said as though in fatal premonition.

There was nothing new to learn from studying the map further. Hector turned and peered hard at the faces of his Platoon leaders. Richard Curry looked terrified.

The Captain drizzled more gloom over the somber mood. "The word coming down from Brigade is that the 'crazies' built their defensive emplacements months ago, as if they anticipated the need for a fall-back position. They'll be ready and waiting for you at sunrise."

Hector smiled thinly, but there was no trace of humor in the expression; just a peeling back of the lips, his face frozen, so that the result was a tight grimace.

The relief-in-place went smoothly, with each platoon on the frontline being replaced in turn by Hector's men. But it was still almost midnight before 'Culprit' Company were finally in position and the exhausted soldiers of the 168th were loaded onto the M-ATVs and heading back towards Seoul.

Hector re-assembled his Platoon leaders together in the shelter of the bunker and was about to pass on his final instructions when a broad-shouldered middle-aged man came through the canvas flap, ducking his head beneath the low entrance.

"Hector?"

The Company officers came to attention but the big man waved the formalities aside with an impatient brush of his hand. "I'm Lieutenant Colonel Wise. I trust you're settling in okay?"

"Yes, sir," Hector said stiffly.

"Good. I'm sure you're all tired, so I'll make this brief," he was a big man who seemed to crowd the available space with the sheer force of his personality. "You know about the assault in the morning. Your men will be one of a dozen line and mechanized Companies, supported by artillery and Abrams tanks. Our objective is to overrun the enemy emplacements between Hill 547 and 581 and then to secure the position and defend it against enemy counter-attacks. We've got one shot at this; the attack must succeed," the Lieutenant Colonel's voice turned grave. "If we can't take and hold that valley in the morning, this whole war is going to bog down and drag out for months. So, we've got to go in hard and fast. Your men fought well at Seoul; you did yourselves proud. I'm glad to have your veterans in the thick of the action," he fired off everything he needed to say in a flurry of short sentences, like a man who needed to be elsewhere. "Any questions?"

"No, sir," Hector said.

"Good. Give 'em hell."

*

An hour before dawn the ground south of the vast network of trenches began to rumble and the air filled with the bellow of hundreds of revving engines. Hector scrambled to the top of the parapet and peered south. The dark skyline was moving; filled with Bradley Fighting Vehicles, Strykers and Abrams tanks that began forming up in the attack position, preparing to join the assault that would commence at first light. Further away he saw five-ton trucks and Humvee support vehicles; an immense armada of steel and firepower gathering to punch through the enemy line like a massive iron fist.

Despite himself, and his misgivings about the assault, the vast swelling bellow of all those engines made Hector's pulse race with a stir of primal fervor.

Men poured from the Brads, milling about like hundreds of ants as the skyline turned pale grey and the first smudge of dawn's clouds became visible, scudding across the horizon as a mist. The dark hulking blur of shapes became sharp silhouettes as the watery daylight grew stronger. Hector stood for a long time, watching the armor assembling; watching the sunrise spill across the churned land and knowing that every passing minute brought him and his men closer to death.

The southern horizon suddenly lit with a fierce orange flicker of winking light, and two seconds later the sky overhead filled with the roar of artillery fire. The shells streaked across the clouds, arcing over Hector's head, and the ground trembled beneath his boots. He spun round and watched the first shells fall. They crashed down two miles to the north in a cacophony of thunderous violence. The explosions flashed red and then burst into billows of smoke, mixing with the morning mist to obscure the devastation they wrought.

The volcanic eruption of smoke and flames turned the valley into a heaving inferno. The Allied artillery roared and raged. The percussion of the heavy guns was like a pummeling of punches so that Hector felt himself physically reel, and the noise became a deafening clamor. A vast cloud of black roiling smoke rolled ponderously across the valley floor, stabbed through with fresh red gouts of flame as each new artillery round crashed and hammered and killed. The torrent of metal being flung at the enemy became unrelenting. The Allied guns were in a rage. The air quivered and grew heated as the two hills that straddled the valley finally took on shape and eminence in the strengthening morning light.

Hector watched the relentless barrage with awe. It seemed impossible that anyone or anything could survive the turmoil of that murderous artillery bombardment. Gayle Nordenman and First Sergeant Ethan Breevor joined him on the lip of the rampart. Nordenman ripped into an MRE, watching the artillery shells continue to pound the enemy's positions like a wide-eyed child viewing 4th of July fireworks. He reached into his pocket and offered one of the ready-to-eat meals to Hector. Hector shook his head. He was too anxious, too on-edge to eat. His stomach was churning with a nauseating witch's brew of emotions.

"Get the men ready," Hector told Breevor. "Any moment now we're going to be ordered forward."

But the attack order did not come. Instead, the sky to the south filled with F-18 Hornet fighter jets. They came out of the clouds and streaked north, whistling overhead and then breaking east and west to drop JDAMs (Joint Direct Attack Munitions) and clusters of laser-guided bombs on the crests of the two hills that stood like sentinels to the gates of the valley.

It seemed to Hector, watching with a sense of hypnotic fascination, that the crest of the hill to the west was cleaved clean off, for it disappeared beneath a vicious, relentless series of massive fireballs. As the flames subsided, the summit of the hill became wreathed behind columns of smoke that obscured it completely from view. More F-18s attacked likely enemy positions atop the eastern hill. A SAM missile streaked out of the smoke and went hunting skywards, chasing the tail of one of the American fighters. The F-18 jinked, ejected a cloud of chaff, and then clawed at the morning sky for altitude. The North Korean missile lost the scent and went fluttering harmlessly across the horizon on a tail of grey vapor.

The fighter jets were followed by a snarl of low-flying A-10 Warthogs. The Hogs came in from the southeast, flying from bases on the outskirts of Seoul. They swept in low, following the contours of the terrain, and disappeared into the thick veil of smoke over the valley, their massive 30mm anti-tank cannons roaring as they strafed the North Korean fixed emplacements. Fresh explosions flared bright through the smoke, and then the Warthogs were peeling away to the west, one of the aircraft trailing a tail of fire and slowly sliding down the sky.

Hector stole a glance back to the south and felt his nerves string tight with a knot of anxiety. The infantry were piling back into their Bradley Fighting Vehicles and Strykers. It was a sure sign the assault was imminent.

Hector gestured with a jut of his chin. "They're mounting up, Gayle."

Nordenman choked down the last of his MRE. Sergeant Breevor returned to the rampart. "The men are ready to rock 'n' roll, sir."

Hector nodded. "Fetch the Platoon leaders, FIST and heavy weapons leaders to the bunker, Sergeant."

Hector wanted to issue final instructions. Now he had seen the mouth of the valley for himself and the rain of fire the artillery had poured onto the enemy's positions, his biggest fear was that the Company would become fragmented in the chaos, the smoke and the confusion of combat.

The Platoon leaders assembled quickly. Their faces were tight with tension.

Hector kept his instructions simple.

"Communications are going to be critical once we reach the enemy's lines," he said. "We don't know exactly what's ahead of us – what to expect. We know there are enemy trenches and emplacements but we don't know the extent of the fortifications or their exact position. So, keep your men together and stay in constant radio comms." He paused for a moment and made eye contact with each person, then went on again, this time directing his instructions pointedly at Lieutenant Curry. "Don't get ahead of the fight and don't lag behind. We go in as a cohesive, coordinated unit and we kill every 'crazy' in front of us. There will be Brads and mech infantry on our flanks. Don't worry about what's happening either side of our unit. Just keep going straight ahead until you run out of enemy to shoot. Hooah."

"Hooah!" everyone in the room responded.

"I want FIST and the heavy weapons squad stuck to me tight as a shadow, understand?" He got eye contact with the Lieutenant leading the Fire Support Team and the Staff Sergeant responsible for the M240 machine guns and the Company's Javelin anti-tank weapons. The FIST Lieutenant was a serious young woman from Indiana. Her features were set, her eyes a little hectic with the prospect of imminent combat. "If I need fire support or if we encounter an enemy tank emplacement, I want to bring the fuckin' noise immediately. Am I clear?"

"Hooah," the Lieutenant and Staff Sergeant responded.

Hector nodded, and took one last look at the strained, grave faces around him. There was nothing more to say. The waiting was over.

Now it was the killing time.

*

The massive Allied artillery bombardment stopped abruptly and the eerie silence following the cacophony of fury was so intense it felt almost painful. The troops of 'Culprit' Company went through their personal pre-combat rituals; compulsively checking their weapons, ammunition and gear, or muttering silent prayers and feeling for the reassurance of lucky charms. Then they screwed up their nerves and went sombrely over the trench parapet and into no-man's land – not in a mad screaming charge, but in a steady line, walking quickly. Out of the corner of Hector's eye he saw Bradley Fighting Vehicles and Abrams tanks moving forward on his flanks. American engineers had excavated wide channels through the North Korean trench network for the armor to pour through and the vehicles dashed forward, churning the long grass to mud and belching clouds of grey exhaust.

The terrain was bumpy and uneven; savaged to cratered ruin by overshot Allied artillery rounds that had pounded the trench line several days earlier during the build-up to the American attack across the DMZ. Now the tanks and APCs were bucking and jouncing through the devastated landscape and for a wry moment, Hector was glad he wasn't one of the mech boys crammed like sardines inside a Brad. He could imagine their discomfort; being thrown about mercilessly like ten-pins within their steel coffins as the fighting vehicles swooped and plunged and swayed.

"Don't bunch up! Curry! Curry! Hold your fuckin' spacing!" Gayle Nordenman bellowed at the rookie Lieutenant. The XO was like a mother hen, keeping the advancing line moving forward in an orderly fashion and making sure the men did not group close together – a common consequence of troops advancing into danger who were inadvertently drawn to each other out of some illusory sense of safety. "Spread the fuck out!"

As they moved forward, the Allied artillery opened up again, this time firing smoke to shield the advance from enemy fire. The rounds landed three hundred yards ahead of the infantry with a muted distinctive *'crump!'* and bloomed into a white swirling curtain of haze.

The column of Brads to the right of the infantry began to accelerate and Hector signalled for his men to keep up. They reached the fogbank of smoke and went through it like they were warily stepping across a threshold into a parallel universe.

On the far side of the smoke, the attack force began funnelling into the mouth of the valley. Through the skeins of haze Hector saw the two hills rising on his flanks as the American attack was forced to compress. The Brads and the Abrams tanks changed course, squeezing towards the center where the infantry were still pushing manfully forward. Hector was struck by a sudden chill premonition of foreboding that ran like a jagged knife down his spine but before he opened his mouth to shout a warning, enemy machine guns opened fire and the world suddenly turned into a blood-soaked inferno.

A man running beside Hector gave a startled groan of pain and then stumbled. Another man folded over slowly, clutching at his stomach. He sank to the ground, his mouth open and gasping, his face blanched of colour and his eyes huge with incredulity.

The smoke haze had concealed a nightmare.

"Keep going! Keep going!" Hector's voice rose above the thunder of enemy gunfire as the men around him began to run and dart and dash forward like dusty spectres. Dripping sweat, their eyes bloodshot, they staggered into the solid wall of enemy defiance. Enemy small arms fire pecked and plucked at the smoke, adding their own throaty hammer to the chaos.

Though outwardly his expression remained fixed and his teeth gritted, Hector's guts were tied in knots and his throat was raw. He aimed his M4 at a stabbing muzzle-flash of flame and fired, then jinked left and flung himself sideways into a shallow scoop of ground as bullets whip-sawed around him. A man staggered through the smoke, his face corpse-like, drained of all colour and masked with mud. His eyes were terrible with fear and despair. "I'm hit!" he croaked. "I'm hit!" He gasped then began to cough up blood. He had been shot under the right arm. He collapsed to the dirt and went into convulsions.

"Medic!" Hector reached for the wounded soldier and dragged him down into the shallow of scant shelter. His hand came away soaked red.

Through a vagary of the wind Hector saw a Bradley away to his right suddenly slew to a halt in the boggy mud and its rear ramp slammed down. A handful of infantry spilled from the vehicle in full battle rattle, their mouths open, shouting, though the sound was lost in the fury of gunfire. Enemy machine guns hunted the troops and bullets clanked sparks off the steel side of the vehicle and then one of the mechanized infantrymen went down and a moment later a flash of light exploded against Hector's eyes as an RPG sizzled through the smoke and struck the Bradley below the turret. The Brad burst into flames, scorching the exterior of the vehicle and shredding the troops sheltering behind its bulk with white-hot chunks of jagged shrapnel. It had all happened in the blink of an eye.

Hector forced himself to his feet and ran on taking hacking, gasping breaths through the choking smoke. Bullets stitched the mud around him and whined about his face. He felt something tug at his arm but when he turned no one was there. He felt his shoulder for wet spots and his fingers came away red and sticky though he felt no pain. A low earth rampart appeared a hundred yards ahead of him through a haze of choking smoke and he opened fire with his M4, shooting from the hip and aiming for the muzzle flashes of the enemy.

Somewhere to the right the sky lit up with a mighty flash of flames and the thunderous roar of an Abrams firing shook the ground. A moment later mortar rounds began exploding, heaving up great gouts of dirt and mud and drifting dust so the haze enveloping the battlefield became impenetrable. Despite his best intentions to keep the Company together, the firefight telescoped down to a few war-torn feet of noise and screams, pain and terror.

He saw dark running shapes to his right, moving like ghosts through the smoke. For a moment he assumed it was 3rd Platoon compressing closer to his position but then he realised they were mechanized infantry dashing towards the enemy rampart surrounded by Bradleys. In the chaos the entire attack had lost its cohesion and he realized the situation was irretrievable.

Now all there was left to do was to fight and kill.

One of the mechanized infantry carrying a SAW went down screaming. Another man snatched for the machine gun and he too was shot down. A third soldier reached for the SAW and picked it up, carrying it cradled in his arms, his head ducked low on his shoulders and his boots scrabbling for purchase in the glutinous mud. The enemy machine guns fired again and the soldier collapsed with his burden, riddled with bullets.

A Brad swerved around a huge shell crater and then exploded into flames and black smoke, struck broadside by an enemy tank. The AFV disintegrated; torn into a thousand flaming steel fragments, killing everyone inside instantly. Ten seconds later a second Brad rocked violently on its tracks from a near miss and then the battlefield seemed to become engulfed in a wave of continuous explosions that filled the searing smoke-filled air with whining shrapnel.

Hector reached the lip of the earthen parapet surrounded by a handful of 2nd Platoon troops and he fired down into the confusion of a deep enemy trench. A grenade exploded. An enemy machine gun roared, cutting down two men. Hector dived head-first into the trench and looked about, wild-eyed. He saw North Korean infantry bodies piled in the bottom of the ditch, some of them dismembered, others dead from ghastly head wounds. The sandbag walls of the trench were slippery and spattered with gore, guts and shredded flesh. The putrid stenches of death and fresh blood mixed with the reek of smoke and sewage to choke in his throat.

More men from 'Culprit' Company tumbled into the trench to join him. He snatched the radio from his RTO (Radio Telephone Operator) and turned his back on the sounds of the battle to shout.

"This is Troublemaker Six to all Troublemaker elements," he called. "Report your positions." With all three Platoons in heavy contact, the Company radio frequency was a nightmare of accidental transmissions of shouting, barked commands, screams of pain and hammering gunfire. Hector waited; his fists clenched as the line hissed with static.

"Troublemaker Six, Troublemaker One-Six. We are in an enemy trench, pinned down by machine gun fire. Multiple casualties and fatalities. Repeat. Multiple injuries and fatalities."

Hector turned, his eyes narrowed. "Curry!" he called the rookie Lieutenant to him. Curry squatted down in the mud at his side. He was breathing hard, almost hyperventilating. His face was caked with mud and scratches and his eyes were huge as saucers.

"1st Platoon is somewhere to the left of us and in this same trench network. Send a squad of men to find them."

Hector tossed the radio back to the RTO. "Let me know when 3rd Platoon reports in. I want to know their location and a SITREP."

The smoke heaved and shifted, shredded by a breeze, and then closed again like a vast theatre curtain, obscuring the battlefield so that the fighting around 'Culprit' Company was revealed only in gruesome snatches. Hector saw the silhouette of an Abrams crash over a low stone wall and then an RPG flashed through the smoke, striking the tank flush on the hull and engulfing it in flames. The Abrams emerged, scorched and blackened, its turret-mounted coax machinegun blazing. Scattered around the tank were dozens of dead bodies; pathetic crumpled, disfigured shapes. Some lay crushed in the mud; some were twisted in cruel attitudes of agony. American and North Korean dead lay slaughtered across the blood-soaked ground like clumps of discarded litter.

Another Bradley emerged through the haze, the hull on fire and trailing smoke. The Brad lurched to a halt just fifty feet from where Hector stood and the rear ramp slammed down. The gunner in the vehicle's turret yanked the charging cable on his M240C coax and began hammering the enemy positions to give covering fire to the handful of mechanized infantry that spilled from the vehicle and came running forward at a crouch, coughing and choking and screaming. Two men were cut down by an enemy mortar round that landed right beside the burning Brad. One soldier froze in mid-stride, his face wrenched into a rictus of agony, and then he arched his back, flung his arms in the air, and fell into the mud. The second man seemed to be suddenly cut off at the knees. His face held a blank look of shock. The M4 he was carrying slipped from his hands and splashed into the mud. He went down in a great gush of blood and rolled onto his back, writhing and twisting as the pain began to rage through him.

"Christ!" John Hector turned away and stared about him in horror. The battle was bogging down, he could sense it. Through the smoke and explosions, he could hear the shouts of wild confusion, the chaos and the clamor of voices edged with shrill panic.

The entire attack teetered precariously on a knife-edge.

Chapter 3:

The remnants of 1st Platoon loomed out of the smoke-filled haze, led by the squad that had gone in search of them. The troops were muddied and bloodied. They had been torn ragged by enemy fire. Medics swarmed over the injured as the battle continued to rage around the trench. Hector knew that to remain still was to invite death; 'Culprit' Company had to maintain their drive forward.

He snatched for the radio again. 3rd Platoon still had not made contact. The net was overwhelmed with shouting, fear-struck voices, competing with each other to be heard through the confusion.

"Clear the fucking net! All Troublemaker elements, clear the god-damned net!" he raged.

Somehow other unit broadcasts were leaking onto the Company's network; voices Hector had never heard before, coming from another part of the battlefield. Lieutenant Colonel Wise's voice added to the garbled confusion, barking orders and urging 'Culprit' Company to push on to the next chain of trenches. Hector only heard half of the instructions.

"Troublemaker One-Three, this is Troublemaker Six. SITREP, for fuck's sake!"

Static warbled over the airwaves in short hissing bursts. Hector threw down the mike, seething with bitter frustration.

He turned and took in the sights and sounds of the raging battle. If he went forward again without 3rd Platoon, he would be charging into the teeth of the enemy's next defensive line with barely half his Company. But if he waited for 3rd Platoon to re-join, he would become prey for the enemy's artillery. He considered sending a squad in search of the missing men, but without some sense of their location, it would be like trying to find a needle in a burning haystack.

The North Koreans made the decision for him.

The rising crescendo of an incoming enemy shell shrieked directly overhead and there was something utterly insidious and chilling about it that made Hector's flesh crawl. He glanced up through the skeins of smoke and a dreadful sense of foreboding sent a frisson of horror down his spine. It was going to land right on top of them.

"Incoming!" he screamed. "Incoming!"

The shell came plummeting out of the sky and Hector had barely enough time to flatten himself against the duckboards in the bottom of the trench. He lay there amongst the stinking gore and twisted swollen entrails of the eviscerated North Korean corpses, waiting for the explosion with his breath jammed in his throat and his frayed nerves strung to snapping point. He could hear his heart thumping in his chest like it was trying to burst free from the cage of his ribs.

The shell struck.

It landed on the lip of the trench, gouging a great crater out of the mire and filling the air with a flail of jagged shrapnel. The ground beneath Hector seemed to heave beneath him and then the sandbagged wall of the trench collapsed, landsliding mud and debris and shattered stumps of wood down upon him. He scrambled out from under the ruins. He could hear a man screaming. He scraped filth from his eyes and turned, his ears ringing. A Corporal from 2nd Platoon stood slumped against a section of crumbled sandbags, his left arm severed above the elbow. Blood was hosing from the wound, soaking his lower body. The soldier stared down at his mutilated arm aghast with shock, his mouth open wide and moving horribly. The medics swarmed over the soldier, and he was lost from Hector's sight behind a wall of bodies.

Hector found Ethan Breevor at the far end of the trench and seized the First Sergeant by the sleeve. "We're moving out," he had to shout above the incessant roar of incoming artillery shells. The North Korean guns and mortars were in a fury. Three more artillery rounds landed within fifty feet of the trench, hurling clods of dirt down on the soldiers of 'Culprit' Company. He dragged the First Sergeant to the lip of the parapet and both men cautiously raised their heads.

Two hundred yards directly in front of them loomed the dark line of another earthen rise. It was veiled in shifting skeins of smoke and punched through with a ragged line of winking muzzle flashes. To their left, Abrams tanks were moving forward cautiously, drifting in and out of the choking veils of haze like prehistoric monsters. To their right Hector could see a unit of mech infantry crawling forward under the hammering cover fire of a line of Bradleys. Mortar shells rained down across the battlefield, and the earth quaked and shook.

"That's the next enemy trench line," Hector pointed ahead. "That's our objective."

"What about 3rd Platoon?"

"We can't fuckin' wait for 'em," Hector growled. "We don't know if they're alive, or even if they've reached this network of trenches. And there's no time to go looking. If we stay here much longer, we're all as good as dead."

Breevor slithered back down into the trench and began bellowing orders. Hector ducked his head as a mortar shell landed nearby, then scanned the battlefield a final time.

A savage roar of tank fire ripped through the black choking smoke. It had come from their left; from somewhere close to the next line of enemy trenches. Hector saw the brilliant fireball of a muzzle flash and then heard a *'clang!'* like a mighty bell tolling. One of the Abrams tanks had taken a close-range hit on its turret and the round had deflected away into the din of the battle. The Abrams returned fire a few seconds later, the muzzle-flash from its barrel lighting up the choking gloom. The sabot round shredded the veil of smoke and struck the enemy tank. The roar of the explosion rolled across the battlefield like a thunderclap and the enemy AFV disappeared behind a sheet of orange flame. Hector watched, transfixed. The mist of smoke parted and through the haze he saw an ancient North Korean T-62 billowing flames. A man appeared in the opening of the sprung turret hatch, his uniform on fire. His hair was burning like a torch and the flesh of his face was melting from the heat, searing away his lips and blistering the skin from his brow. The burning ghoul clawed at the air and the screech of terror torn from his lungs was filled with all the horror and excruciating agony that a man could ever endure.

He tried to drag himself free of the inferno, but the flames engulfed him, and he slipped back down into the blazing hull.

The Abrams fired again, this time striking the T-62 flush on the hull. The round tore through the North Korean vehicle's layer of protective armor and the tank blew apart with such ferocity that the turret was wrenched clean off the T-62 and flung cartwheeling through the smoke on a comet's tail of sparks and fire.

"The men are ready!" Breevor threw himself back down in the mud beside Hector. The Sergeant's voice sounded oddly calm despite the maelstrom of fighting. Hector gritted his teeth. He again peered right. The mech infantry crawling forward through the mud were coming under light arms fire and a downpour of mortar shells. One of the Brads providing overwatch for the attack was struck by an RPG and became engulfed in flames.

Hector peered over his shoulder and stared down at the men who were lined along the wall of the trench, looking up at him with fixed grimaces, waiting for his order. He felt himself tense, the muscles in his thighs bunching like a runner on the starting blocks. He slapped a fresh magazine into his M4 and crushed down savagely on the rising wave of his panic.

"Go! Go! Go!" he filled his lungs then roared, scrambling to his feet and running headlong into the terrible carnage of the killing ground.

*

Hector shouted an incoherent cry of rage; rage and hatred and fear. He fired from the hip as he ran, aiming for the muzzle flashes that winked and spat at him. The men were at his side and they were shouting with the same indistinguishable primal roar, their legs pumping, their boots slipping and sliding in the crater-torn mud.

A man to Hector's right staggered and then seemed to sag to the ground in slow motion, his brow furrowed in confusion because one of his legs was missing. A Corporal swayed like a boxer as bullets whiplashed around him. He took two steps forward, ducked, weaved, and then was suddenly lifted off his feet and slammed back into the mud by the impact of an enemy bullet. He cried out in agony then rolled onto his stomach and began to sob pitifully. The rest of the Company ran past him, each man enduring his own private hell. Sergeant Penway from 1st Platoon paused on a small muddy rise and turned to urge his men forward. Enemy bullets howled and fizzed past his ear. "Move your fuckin' asses!" he roared. Two more men cried out, the breath slamming in their throats. Choking smoke billowed in thick swirling clouds, turning the distant trench line into a vague shifting shape without clear definition, and painting pale halos of light around the muzzle flashes of the enemy machine guns. Penway fired into the mist and then was shot in the face. The savage impact of the bullet snapped his chin back and his helmet went spinning through the air. His head collapsed and the contents of his skull dissolved into grey mist. The corpse went tumbling face-first into the mud.

Thirty yards short of the trench, Hector dived into a shallow crater of torn earth and pressed his face into the dirt as a hail of enemy bullets plucked and ripped at the earth around him. The air was heated and flailed by the incessant *'crump!'* of incoming mortar rounds and the flaming roar of the firefight. He turned his head slightly and saw Sergeant Breevor still running forward, stooped low like a man leaning into the teeth of a howling gale. He had a grenade in his hand and as Hector watched, Breevor hurled the missile towards the enemy trench. It fell short and exploded in a shroud of flung dirt and debris.

Hector sucked in two deep breaths and pushed himself to his feet. He could see the enemy parapet clearly through the smoke now; a low rise of earth that had been reinforced by a retaining wall of logs. Lined along the lip of the emplacement were dozens of North Korean soldiers, their heads and shoulders just visible, their weapons spitting death and flame from close range. They were backlit like silhouettes by a flicker of orange light from the North Korean artillery batteries, still pounding the Allied advance.

Hector snatched for a grenade and threw it ahead of him. The explosion echoed dull and distant and he knew he had missed the trench. He cursed bitterly under his breath and fired with a fresh magazine in his M4. The roar of a SAW somewhere in the smoke drowned out the chatter of his weapon but he saw his rounds fly wide and he cursed again. Then the hammer of the SAW cut a swath along the lip of the parapet, chewing splinters of wood from the wall and knocking down enemy soldiers in spurts and spatters of blood. Hector heard tight screams of pain, and he growled savagely.

"Charge the fuckers!"

He seemed suddenly filled with fresh energy and his mind went mercifully blank. The fear dropped away from him, the cataclysmic roar of combat faded, and the smoke shroud parted to reveal a clear path to the enemy trench. He ran like a man pursued by the devil, and with him went a dozen others, screaming like fiends and swearing their fury.

An enemy bullet flew past his face, its passage so close to his cheek that he felt the buffet of heated air and staggered. Then he was up again, snarling savage, unholy retribution. Grenades exploded and a man screamed. Hector reached the lip of the trench, swung his M4 down into the dark void, and emptied a full magazine. A North Korean soldier was punched back against a sandbagged wall. His corpse jinked and twitched with each flailing impact until the bullet-riddled body slumped down into the mud. Another enemy soldier came shouting out of the smoke from the left. Hector turned, saw the man wielding some kind of weapon and instead of trying to reload, he reversed the carbine in his hands and leaped down into the litter of shattered bodies, swinging the stock of the M4 like an axe. The North Korean soldier ran straight into the wicked arc of the weapon and was struck in the face. The impact shattered his jaw and flung him sideways, blood gushing from the mangled ruin of his mouth. Hector threw down the M4 and went forward snarling, arms outstretched, fingers hooked like claws. He was twenty pounds heavier than the enemy soldier and four inches taller. He piledrove the North Korean hard against a wall of blood-spattered sandbags and wrapped his hands around the other man's throat, wringing his neck.

More men from 'Culprit' Company leaped down into the trench. A band of North Koreans counter-attacked from the right. They swarmed over the duckboards in a knot, screaming with maniacal frenzy. Sergeant Breevor went forward to meet them, his carbine on his hip and his lip curled into a cruel snarl of disdain. The M4 roared, the shadow-struck trench lit with the hammering muzzle-flash, and the enemy soldiers went down in a bloody tangle of writhing agony.

"Check left!" Hector sent two men to the end on the trench section where the excavation suddenly jagged away at an angle. He sent two more men past the steaming heap of torn flesh Breevor had just piled high on the duckboards. The two soldiers clambered over the broken remains of the enemy soldiers. A North Korean was still alive, his cries for help feeble and strained, coming from within the jumble of corpses. A shot rang out; a single echo amongst the thousands that were criss-crossing the battlefield – and the enemy soldier's pleas for mercy were cut abruptly short.

From the right came a flurry of shouted voices and then suddenly, miraculously, the ragged remains of 3rd Platoon appeared through the smoke and fire. They were haggard, battle-scarred wraiths in the black sifting haze. They appeared, led by their Sergeant, carrying several wounded between them. They dropped down into the trench, their expressions haunted, their eyes made vacant by all the horror they had endured. Somehow, two mech infantry had joined their ranks after becoming separated from their own unit.

"Where's Threllfall?" Hector did a silent headcount of the 3rd Platoon survivors and was appalled. Only twenty-seven men remained, and four of them were out of the fight with serious wounds.

"The Lieutenant's dead," the Platoon Sergeant said. The Sergeant was a veteran of the war in Afghanistan, a good, steady soldier from Montana who walked and talked like a wild west cowboy and was a brute in a fight. "Grenade got him."

Hector nodded, but asked no more questions. The time for enquiries, regrets and remorse would come after the fighting and killing.

He scrambled up the wall of the trench and lifted his head cautiously. All around their small crater-strewn piece of the battlefield the fighting still raged. It seemed as if the world was in a maddened frenzy. Artillery rounds fell like rain, overlaid by the more muted *'crump!'* of falling mortar shells, while to his left more Abrams tanks were heavily engaging North Korean armor, the wicked crack of sabot rounds trembling the air. To the right of the Company the battle was in a lull; a brief battlefield phenomenon of seeming silence, even though the fighting still raged and the sky was rimmed with flames and the charred mangled ruins of Bradley Fighting Vehicles.

Then, from out of the grey smoke, a sudden hammer of heavy machine gun fire plucked and ripped at the ground around Hector's face. It had come from somewhere ahead of him; a savage thundering crescendo of new death. He slithered down into cover and clamped his hands over his head, his face buried in the mud until the storm of bullets subsided, then he peered wild-eyed back into the wall of smoke.

He could see nothing but mud and blood and bodies.

The heavy machine gun roared again and this time Hector caught a glimpse of flaming muzzle flash before the ground was shredded about him again and he ducked behind cover.

"HMG," Hector warned Breevor who had crawled close beside him. "It's ahead of us, and off to our left about a hundred yards," he identified the enemy position. "We're not going any further until we can take the fucker out."

The two men slid back down into the bottom of the trench and shouldered their way fifty yards along the duckboards, wading through the milling, exhausted men. When they clambered up the revetment again, the enemy machine gun was directly ahead, still firing at an oblique angle, catching unsuspecting American troops blundering through the smoke of no-man's land in a lethal enfilade.

Hector peered hard. The smoke drifted in thick layers, ripped apart by falling mortar rounds and upheaved gouts of flung dirt.

"It's the shape and size of an old T-54 tank turret," Hector's eyes burned from the fumes and smoke. The bunker was topped by a rounded cupola and constructed from thick concrete, reinforced with iron. As he watched, the HMG mounted within the emplacement roared again, spitting flames and carnage. The gun was sited in a narrow steel-framed embrasure with a field of fire that covered the entire sector of trenches

"You wanna call up the arty?" Breevor considered the options.

Hector shook his head. From the corner of his eye, through the black smoke, he saw a handful of American soldiers suddenly emerge from out of the trench and go running across no-man's land, heading towards some unseen objective in the distance. They ran hunched over, their mouths open and shouting, though the sounds of their voices was drowned out. But Hector could see the tight strain in their mud-spattered bodies; the fear and desperation driving them forward. Then the North Korean machine gun in the bunker roared and the Americans went down in a heap, slaughtered to a man.

"Fuckers!" Hector snarled. He cast about him in desperation but could see no solution. The Abrams tanks were further to their left and seemed to be stalled in their advance. "Fuck it!" he growled. "We're going to take the bastard out ourselves."

He slid down into the depths of the trench, his jaw clenched and his mood resolved. He hand-picked fifteen men, all of them experienced combat veterans he knew and trusted, and pulled them into a huddle while the artillery rounds continued to rain down around them.

"Three teams of five" he explained quickly. "Go left, go right, and then we drive forward through the center, grenades in hand. Understand?" he scraped a diagram in the mud at their feet, indicating the role of each knot of men. Everyone nodded, grimly aware that some of them were about to die, and then they broke into their groups and scurried to their positions.

Hector gave the signal and five men went over the lip of the trench, screaming. They circled left of the emplacement and the moment they emerged through the smoke the enemy machine gun hunted them.

"Go! Go! Go!" Hector cried.

Five more men burst into no-man's land and swept right, using the uneven crater-strewn ground and the thick choking haze to mask their advance. The enemy machine gun swung across an arc of almost ninety degrees and the evil flickering tongue of its muzzle flash winked and spat venom.

"Now!"

Ethan Breevor led the five-man attack team. They heaved themselves up out of the trench and ran straight for the emplacement, the tough Sergeant in the lead and the rest of the men running hard to keep pace with him. They were just thirty yards short of the bunker when the gunners serving the North Korean HMG recognized the threat. The machine gun swung and a ragged line of chattering death moved over the ground, hunting the Americans. Breevor jinked left, ducked, and then threw himself down into the mud like a man diving under the blade of a giant scythe. The moment he sensed the bullets had swept past him he was on his feet again, fury driving him, fear and fierce pride propelling him forward. Two of his team were down. He caught sight of one man's death throes as he fell, but Breevor kept on charging ahead. His legs felt like lead weights. His thighs were burning and his lungs were on fire. He reached the emplacement and slammed into the cold thick dome of concrete gasping and heaving, his whole body gripped in uncontrollable spasms of exhilaration and terror. He dropped down to his knees. He could see the emplacement's slit embrasure just a yard from where he knelt.

The machine gun was blazing, the roar deafening. He could feel the heat from the muzzle flash and actually see the end of the barrel as it traversed onto a new target.

Breevor unclipped two grenades from his webbing and tossed them through the narrow embrasure. The machine gun suddenly stopped firing and the American heard two startled North Korean voices. The enemy soldiers' words were unintelligible, but the panic in their tone was unmistakable.

"Choke on that you fuckers!" Breevor snarled. A split second later the grenades exploded and a plume of black sooty smoke erupted through the embrasure. The ground beneath Breevor's feet seemed to leap and shudder. He slumped against the cold concrete wall, the rage that had carried him suicidally into the teeth of enemy fire suddenly replaced by grim satisfaction and a rush of violent trembles.

'Culprit' Company burst from the trench with Hector leading them and dashed forward. All along the line, the Americans were on the move and the North Koreans were finally in retreat. A Battalion artillery barrage chased the enemy, snapping at their heels as they fell back through the veils of smoke.

It wasn't quite over, but nearly so.

Pockets of North Korean resistance continued to fight for another hour before being overrun or surrendering. By midday the valley had been seized by the Americans, the North Koreans had been thrown back in retreat, and now the route to Kaesong lay undefended and open for the next phase of the Allied advance.

*

There were bodies everywhere.

The dead were strewn across the crater-churned fields and lay buried in the glutinous mud. They were piled in drifts around the blackened twisted wreckage of destroyed tanks, and they were bundled in stinking heaps along the length of the trenches. They had been thrown down in droves where the fighting had been the fiercest and left scattered in small groups in places where only the artillery had reached. Men had been shredded by shrapnel, disfigured by explosions and flailed by gunfire.

For miles in every direction, the battlefield was a slaughteryard of blood and guts and gore, steaming in the warm afternoon air.

Here and there, moving in shambles and staggers, the survivors began to emerge. They drifted out of the smoke, or crawled from beneath the piles of bloating fly-blown corpses. One man got to his feet, numb and silently screaming because he was splattered in his buddy's guts. Another crawled from the cavity of a bomb crater seemingly unscathed until he looked down and saw his entrails spilling from his stomach and dragging in the mud behind him. A Sergeant, his forearm hanging from his elbow by just the tattered remains of his uniform and a few shreds of flesh, reached for the side of a Bradley Fighting Vehicle to hold himself upright, and then began to softly weep.

A convoy of mud-spattered ambulances reached the front and a small army of medics went to work on the maimed and dying. Black Hawks hung in the air to the south of the valley, flying non-stop relay routes between the battlefront and the field hospitals on the outskirts of Seoul. A Casualty collection point was established, but so overwhelming were the numbers of dead and dying that a second casualty site had to be established. In the afternoon, a fleet of bulldozers arrived and began the grim task of digging mass graves.

The air stank of smoke and corruption. Many of the bodies had begun to bloat and turn purple in the humid heat. Flies hung in black swarming clouds, laying their eggs in open mouths and eye cavities while the living drifted around the battlefield like the stunned survivors of a holocaust.

One of the mech infantrymen that had fought on the right flank of 'Culprit' Company during the attack wandered through the North Korean dead searching the mutilated bodies for cigarettes. An enemy soldier suddenly groaned and gasped a despairing plea for water. The North Korean's chest had been cleaved open by shrapnel, exposing white shards of broken rib bones and the bloody gore of his guts.

"Do you have cigarettes, you crazy fucker?" the American rifled the man's pockets and found a crumpled half-packet. Then he clamped his hand over the dying North Korean's mouth and held it there until the feeble struggles ended and the enemy soldier lay completely still.

In the middle of the afternoon the rain came again. It began as a mist of drifting showers and then became a downpour that filled the craters and trench line with puddles of water and washed away the blood. Exhausted men tried to sleep. Some crawled under the hulls of the tanks and parked AFVs for shelter. Others simply slumped down into the quagmire and closed their eyes. A few men, unable to rest and still haunted by the horror they had endured, sat in small knots, miserable and vacant-eyed, staring into empty space.

John Hector sat propped on an upended ammunition box and watched a woman on a stretcher being loaded into the back of a Humvee by two medics. The wounded soldier was a specialist from 1st Platoon. She had been shot in the neck during the last few moments of fighting. All he could see of her was a tress of blood-soaked blonde hair and a glimpse of her pale face. He waited until the Humvee went skidding away in the mud and then pushed himself stiffly to his feet.

The Company was north of the second enemy trench line, in the muddy morass around the enemy bunker that Ethan Breevor had disabled with grenades. The emplacement had been a two-man machine gun position, connected to a network of other similar bunkers by narrow tunnels. Now the bunkers were all silent and blackened, and the tunnel network had been collapsed by American engineers, leaving the terrain cut with a maze of caved-in ditches.

Hector saw Richard Curry walking through the mire towards him. The Lieutenant's face was pale. Curry stopped suddenly and looked down, then shuddered when he realized he was standing in the tangled blue dribble of someone's guts. He crossed himself as if to apologise to his God, and then kept walking, his features grave and fixed as though he were stifling a scream.

"You've got a butcher's bill, Lieutenant?" It seemed to take a great effort for Hector to muster the strength even to ask the question. He was so physically exhausted, and so wrung out by the anxiety of combat that he could barely rouse the energy to lift his head.

"Sir?"

"How many dead? How many wounded?"

"Eleven dead, sir. Another nine wounded. Half the Platoon…"

"Christ!" Hector stiffened and stared in horror. The casualty counts from the other two Platoons had been similar. 'Culprit' Company had been decimated – reduced to half strength in just a few furious hours of savage fighting. Maybe a third of the casualties would eventually return to the front. The rest were destined for a muddy grave or a hospital gurney.

Curry spun on his heel and went traipsing away into the battle-torn landscape. Gayle Nordenman brought Hector a mug of hot coffee from an aid station tent that was dispensing MREs and Styrofoam cups of coffee to a long line of bedraggled haggard survivors. The XO's cheek twitched and the hand that carried the coffee mug was shaking.

"I'm reconsidering my career choice," the XO said lightly, though his eyes were dark and troubled and his expression earnest. Nordenman had been in the thick of the fighting. A Corporal from 2nd Platoon had died screaming in his arms from a bullet wound to the head. The XO had nursed the man, holding his shattered skull together with his bloody hands and pleading for a medic that never arrived.

"Me too," Hector accepted the coffee with a nod of thanks and peered across the muddy carnage from over the rim of the steaming mug. Trees had been shredded of their leaves and the slopes of the two hills had been denuded of grass cover.

The landscape looked like a vast open-cut mine; a brown hideous scar on the face of the world.

Hector felt stiff as an old man and his breath came in a sob. He started walking towards the destroyed North Korean bunker and the men of 'Culprit' Company watched him hobble past from behind blackened mud-spattered faces.

Hector went around to the far side of the concrete dome, out of sight, and quietly threw up.

Chapter 4:

Two ROKAF F-16 Fighting Falcons went streaking across the sky, flying high and heading north, bristling with bombs beneath their wings. Hector watched the fighters until they disappeared from sight, and then turned his attention back to his small corner of the battlefield.

The captured North Korean trenches were swarming with Intelligence officers searching for documents, and teams of bomb-disposal experts who probed for booby-traps. No-man's land – between the first and second line of enemy fortifications – was now filling with mess tents to feed the exhausted troops, while in the distance, still far to the south but coming closer, Hector could see a long unwieldly column of M-ATVs heading in his direction. The vehicles were making hard work of the crater-churned mud, struggling to maintain momentum and formation.

"Reinforcements?" Gayle Nordenman guessed, nodding in the direction of the approaching trucks. He had appeared at Hector's shoulder suddenly.

Hector grunted. "Maybe..." he acknowledged. "We could have used the fuckers an hour ago..."

A young medic, pale-faced and his features lined with fatigue, wandered past and stopped suddenly. "You've been shot, sir." He pointed at Hector's left arm.

"It's just a graze," Hector fingered the wound on his shoulder. A North Korean bullet had torn a hole in the sleeve of his uniform and nicked the flesh of his bicep. Hector could barely remember the moment it had happened.

The medic fished around for antiseptic and a bandage and strapped the wound then hurried off without another word. Hector felt vaguely embarrassed. All around him were rows of stretchers bearing the maimed and dying who were awaiting evac to Seoul. His flesh wound hardly seemed worthy of attention considering the far greater sacrifice of those men. He waited until the medic began tending the injured foot of another soldier and he tore the bandage off.

The column of approaching vehicles finally reached the rim of the valley and plunged forward, following a rutted path worn in the mud by Abrams tanks, splashing and jouncing across the churned terrain. The lead vehicle crawled past Hector and he recognized the faces of the men instantly. He turned to Nordenman with a look of bitter resentment. "It's the rest of the Battalion," Hector said. "Fucking typical."

The M-ATVs and a handful of M1083s rolled by, the men in the back of the vehicles gawking with shock and appalled disbelief at the carnage of the battlefield. A soldier from 'Culprit' Company jeered the arriving troops, his voice full of scorn and bitter recrimination. "Where were you, you bastards?" he spat in the mud as one of the trucks splashed past him. "Where the fuck were you when the bullets were flying and we were being slaughtered?"

The taunts were taken up by others in the Company and soon the replacement troops were driving through a torrent of insults and savage recrimination. It was more than heckling; there was something almost frenetic in the abuse, being hurled by men who had been to the very edge of the abyss and returned forever haunted.

One of the M-ATVs pulled off to the side of the track and Lieutenant Colonel Benedict Gallman climbed down from the passenger side of the vehicle. He was wearing a clean, freshly-pressed uniform. In one of his hands he held a map, clutched tightly between his long tapered fingers. He turned in a slow circle, his eyes taking in the miles of devastated terrain, the graveyard of smoldering, ruined vehicles, and the long rows of wounded laying on stretchers.

"You should go and make a report," Nordenman urged Hector.

"Fuck him. He's nothing but a fucking REMF (Rear Echelon Mother Fucker)," Hector spat. "If Gallman wants me, he'll find me. And besides, we're still attached to the 168th, so it's Colonel Wise I'll make my report to, not this stuffed-shirt fucking show pony."

Nordenman made a wry face. "Well by the looks of things, I think we're back with the Battalion, because Gallman is coming this way."

"Hector?"

John Hector turned slowly. "Sir?"

Gallman stopped short of Hector and a flinch of shock rippled over the senior officer's face. Hector's uniform was covered with dried gore, blood and mud. His face was haggard and his eyes were red-rimmed and sunk deep into their sockets. He reeked of smoke and vomit and sweat.

"It was a hard fight, I'm told," Gallman made a feeble attempt at conversation.

Hector swatted the Colonel down brutally. "It was, sir. A lot of men died, and a lot more were seriously wounded. In all the battles I've been at the frontline fighting since we arrived in country, this was the hardest." Gallman hadn't been within a mile of enemy gunfire since the Battalion had shipped to South Korea in the weeks leading up to the Battle of Seoul.

Gallman's thin smile turned frosty. Hector's pointed barb had not passed unnoticed. The Colonel sniffed, then peered past Hector and swept his eyes across the troops of 'Culprit' Company who were still jeering and hurling abuse at the rest of the arriving Battalion. Gallman deliberately chose to blindly ignore the defiant shouting rather than have his authority tested. He had little doubt that if he ordered the 'Culprits' to cease their taunting, they would blatantly ignore his command. So instead, he cast aside any pretence of familiarity and thrust out his chin.

"You have new orders, Captain," he said. "Your Company is now re-attached to 9th Battalion and under my command. Your men will be moving out in an hour's time. Your mission is to secure a hill three miles north of here," he unfurled the map and spread it over the bonnet of the Oshkosh. Hector, sullen and defiant, refused to look. He was incensed with rage and frustration. Gallman went on regardless, wanting to get through the briefing as quickly as possible. He could sense Hector's seething hostility.

"The hill is known as 'Little Janice'. It is one of three low rises north of the valley. Your Company will secure the hilltop and hold that position until dawn tomorrow. You will be one of three picquet units protecting the Army from an enemy counter-attack during the night. At dawn, the rest of the Battalion will move up to reinforce you and begin preparations for the assault on Kaesong."

"Sir," Hector spat the honorific in a snarl. "My men are exhausted. They've been fighting the enemy since sunrise. Almost half of my Company are either dead or wounded. They need rest. They need a decent hot meal and ten hours sleep. They need a fucking shower and a shave to wash the mud and shit and blood and guts off them."

Gallman stood like a statue as Hector's tirade battered him. The Colonel gave another arrogant self-important thrust of his chin and lifted his head a little so that he was staring over Hector when he replied, averting the accusation in the other man's eyes.

"We all have to make sacrifices, Captain," he said icily. "There's a war going on, and it can't be conducted only when it suits you."

"Surely another Company can stand picquet."

"No," Gallman shook his head. "Tomorrow the entire Battalion will be engaged in the drive for Kaesong. Your Company is the only one that is already forward and prepared to move out. It has to be 'Culprit' Company, and you have to be atop 'Little Janice' and dug in before dark."

"But, sir –"

"You're dismissed, Captain," Gallman turned on his heel. He climbed quickly back into the Oshkosh and snapped at the driver. "Get me out of here. Now!"

*

"The fucking asshole!" Hector raged; his face twisted into an ugly, indignant snarl. "The fucking cock-sucking REMF ass-kissing fucking piece of shit!" He turned and drove his fist into the steel side of a nearby parked M-ATV and then instantly regretted it. A white-hot lance of pain shot up his arm and his hand came away bloody, but it did not diffuse his anger. He was in a towering rage; a savage blazing volcano of foul fury.

Gayle Nordenman waited patiently for Hector's eruption of anger to turn into simmering frustration before he spoke. He was just as furious as his Captain, but Nordenman's temperament was less volatile.

"Do you want me to assemble the command team?"

Hector's mouth was pinched into a bloodless pale line, his brows knotted together, and his jaw clenched. "Yes."

The Platoon leaders and their Sergeants assembled in the mud by the side of the track leading north. Hector passed on his orders in short, clipped sentences so his bitterness was apparent to everyone. Richard Curry listened with a mixture of dismay and umbrage. Finally, Hector finished relaying their new orders with a sigh and a weary shake of his head.

"So that's it," he growled. "Gallman, the piss-faced asshole, wants us dug in on top of 'Little Janice' before nightfall. Inform your men. Tell them to grab all the ammunition they can lay their hands on. The M-ATVs will be pulling out in an hour."

The group dispersed, heading towards the waiting troops, moving like cops about to deliver bad news to the relatives of a murder victim. Lieutenant Curry waited until he was alone with Hector and Nordenman before he spoke.

"Sir, I find your disrespect to the Lieutenant Colonel offensive," he announced stiffly, his back straight but his hands trembling. "I feel it's unbecoming of an officer to speak with contempt about his superior."

Hector arched his eyebrows and flicked a bemused glance at Gayle Nordenman. He stared for an incredulous moment at the rookie Lieutenant and the XO tensed, expecting that any moment John Hector would go for the younger man's throat and tear his heart out through his asshole.

"What did you say?" Hector's voice dropped to a menacing whisper.

"I... I said I find it unbecoming to speak of a senior officer of the United States Army in such derogatory terms," the defiant rookie stood his ground. He was sweating, melting under the blazing fury in Hector's eyes. His sense of respect for authority that had been drilled into him during IOBC at Fort Benning was the foundation of his military belief system; the unwavering faith in the chain of command and the authority of senior officers.

"You listen to me," Hector took a dangerous step closer to Curry and his eyes flashed like the edge of an unsheathed dagger. "I've been fighting this war since before the Battle of Seoul. I've been knee-deep in mud and fucking blood and fucking guts without a rest for weeks. I've seen good men maimed and heroes killed. I've seen innocent civilians slaughtered and burned alive. And in all that time, I've never once seen Lieutenant Colonel Gallman. He spends his time at the rear, issuing orders. The only time he appears is after a battle, when the bullets stop flying – and then it's only to take credit for our sacrifice and to kiss the ass of the Brigade Commander," Hector paused just long enough to take a snarl of breath. "You find my fucking language offensive, Lieutenant? Well, I find Gallman offensive. He's a cowardly prick who doesn't know the first thing about real leadership or the meaning of valor. Report me if you want – I don't give a fuck. But until I'm hauled away in cuffs, I'm still the Captain of this Company and you're a Lieutenant under my command. So shut your fucking mouth until you've been spattered in blood and drenched in a man's guts. When you've held the hand of a soldier who is bleeding out and sobbing for his mother, then you can lecture me about respect. Until then, fuck off!"

Curry stood rigid throughout Hector's tirade like a man standing in the face of a thunderstorm.

"Yes, sir." He stiffened, and then turned smartly on his heel, his legs threatening to collapse under him as he walked away, so feverish was his shaking.

Hector watched the Lieutenant slosh through the mud towards the survivors of 2nd Platoon.

"Plucky little bastard," Gayle Nordenman grunted. "That took some balls."

"Yeah," Hector's temper had blown itself out, and now he just felt impossibly tired; wearier and more worn down than at any other time of his life. "If he doesn't get himself killed, he might just make a half-decent officer," he conceded with grudging regard.

*

M-ATVs transported the weary survivors of 'Culprit' Company to the southern slope of 'Little Janice' and dumped the troops unceremoniously at the foot of the escarpment. The men unpacked their equipment, grumbling and sullen, and then began the long trudge up the face of the rise.

The hill was a two-hundred-foot-high gentle slope of grass and tree covered elevated ground, crowned by a bald granite dome of black rock. Hector stood atop the hillock and turned in a slow circle.

The view south to the battlefield in the valley was obscured by a thick pall of black smoke that spread like a dark scar across the horizon. Amidst the swirling cloud, Hector could still see pinpricks of red flaring light from burning tanks.

To the east and west of their location, the land was a vista of undulating hills cut through with narrow valley gorges. The land was lush and green – almost jungle-like in some places. Here and there small patches of land had been cleared and cultivated by local peasants for farming. Hector pressed binoculars to his eyes and focussed his attention to the north.

Somewhere in that vast expanse of darkening landscape was the retreating North Korean Army, but when he looked for tell-tale traces, he could see nothing in the dusk. It was ideal terrain to hide in, he realized. The hills and valleys gave good concealment and would prove perfect locations to obscure ambushes. Hector pitied the poor bastards who would be leading the Allied Army's advance towards Kaesong. The drive north would be a nightmare of enemy assaults, skirmishes and RPG attacks along narrow valleys, hemmed in on both sides by densely wooded terrain from where the enemy would be well concealed. It was insurgent territory, and if the North Koreans had any sense – and Hector knew the enemy were not stupid – they would fight a guerrilla campaign, terrorising the Allies and making them pay dearly for every mile they captured.

Most probably, Hector decided, the Allies would push forward behind Abrams tanks and under the cover of swooping Apache attack helicopters, but in ambush country the advantages of the American's advanced hardware could be entirely negated by a well-located IED and a couple of men with RPGs or anti-tank guns.

Sergeant Breevor seemed to read Hector's thoughts. "Makes you glad you ain't a tanker, right?"

"Roger that," Hector grunted with feeling.

He turned and cast his eyes across the hilltop. The ground was barren black rock outcrops surrounded on all sides by a fringe of long grass. Hector winced. It was an ugly place to defend; the men could not entrench themselves amongst the rocks but would be forced to take up positions down the slope in the grass – and that would mean a dispersed and over-extended perimeter.

Again, it seemed that Breevor was ahead of him. The Sergeant shoved an MRE into his open mouth and gnawed at the end of it, talking around the ration with his mouth full.

"Reckon we set 1st Platoon to the east, 3rd Platoon to the west, and you keep 2nd Platoon close to you. The new Lieutenant still ain't pissin' yellow and he's likely to get skittish if the 'crazies' come. Might be good to have him close to you. We could set the mortars and MGs up in the rocks to overwatch the Platoon positions…"

Hector nodded. It was as good a plan as any. "Make it happen," he agreed. "But I want the heavy weapons behind some cover. If there isn't enough natural shelter amongst the boulders, get them stacking rocks around their gear. If the 'crazies' do attack, it will be under a barrage of mortar fire, so I want all the cover for our guys we can get."

Breevor went to work, bellowing and shouting men into action, his voice cracking like a whip. Hector and Gayle Nordenman went down the northern slope of the hill, wading through the long grass and trees.

"Claymores here," Hector ran a soldier's eye over the terrain. The hillside was cut through with deep trenches from rain runoff, and each rain-worn ravine offered enemy concealment. "If they come in the night, they'll use these dry beds to close on our position, so I want it all mined, Gene. And I want tripwires and flares, okay?"

Nordenman nodded. "You think an attack is likely?"

Hector shrugged. "Typically, no," he said after a long moment of thought. "They should be broken. They should be miles from here, falling back on Kaesong. But we don't call them 'crazies' for nothing. The first rule of warfare is to do what the enemy doesn't want and expects least."

Nordenman looked troubled. A bleak, pessimistic man at the best of times, he frowned and lowered his voice, as though what he was about to say was almost unpatriotic. "If they do attack, John, and if they come at us in numbers, we're not in great shape to hold them off, y'know?"

"I know," Hector said. The Company was barely at half strength and exhausted from a full day of brutal combat. The 'Culprits' were vulnerable and exposed – and both officers knew it. "What have we got for fire support if we have to call in the arty?"

"Paladins from Charlie Battery, 113th Field Artillery, 30th Armored Brigade Combat Team."

"Has our FIST set up direct comms links?"

"It's done," Nordenman nodded.

"Good. Let's pray we don't need them."

They started back up the slope. At the fringe of the grass, where it gave way suddenly to bare rock, men were stripped to the waist digging foxholes and filling sandbags with the displaced dirt. Hector paused to chivvy and joke with a couple of men, then strode on, his eyes seemingly everywhere at once. On a boulder near the crown of the hill, someone had found time to whitewash a sign across the face of the granite slab.

'Little Big Horn. Hector's last stand.'

Hector saw the sign and grinned mirthlessly with the macabre black humor that every soldier needed to survive the gruesome horrors of war.

"As soon as the Claymores are laid and the trenches dug, I want everyone to get some food in their guts. We'll post half the men on sentry duty and let the others sleep," Hector said. "Two hour shifts until sunrise, and pray for a quiet night."

"Amen to that," Gayle Nordenman said with feeling.

*

Hector lay stretched out on a slab of rock and worried. He could hear around him the soft sounds of other men sleeping; a muted phlegmy cough, the sawing of a snore, a name called in the night, the stirring of bodies tossing and turning.

But Hector could not sleep. He lay on his back with one arm under his head as a pillow and a cigarette in his free hand. He stared up at the star-filled night. Smoke and clouds were drifting across the sky. The events of the battle in the valley ran through his mind like disjointed images played through a projector: the graphic recollection of men dying, the dreadful sounds of screaming, and the pounding of the artillery, like endless jungle drums. He saw men's faces – men who were now dead – and he saw their terrible anguish as they fell bleeding and broken to the ground. The taste of his fear came back into his throat and he drew deeply on the cigarette but the taint lingered. He sat up because he couldn't bear the horror of remembering for a moment longer.

He stared out into the still night. His mind began to conjure up fantasies from the darkness. The distant silhouette of a tree further down the slope became a running North Korean soldier and a clump of bush transformed into the vague shape of an enemy mortar team.

Hector's breath scratched in his throat, and he felt his stomach knot. He looked away to the east for a long moment, then turned back. The tree was gone…

A hand shot out of the night and clamped like a vice on Hector's wrist. He jerked into instant alertness.

"The fuckers are coming," Sergeant Breevor pressed his mouth close and whispered the warning, his voice hoarse and urgent. "I can hear them. They're down the northern slope a couple of hundred yards away."

Hector nodded. "Alert the men – quietly."

Breevor ghosted away, moving like a wraith and Hector slid off the rock and moved stealthily to where the Company mortars and the two M240 machine guns were set up. The machine guns were positioned so that one gun covered the eastern flank and the other gun covered the western flank, with both weapons on bipods, capable of covering an attack from the north. Between them were situated the two 60mm mortars. The Staff Sergeant commanding the mortars was on sentry duty. Hector crept quietly to his side.

"Enemy, down the slope. Get everyone up and ready, but do it quietly."

Hector peered back down the northern slope of the hill. The night remained tense and silent. Nothing moved, and for a moment he wondered if Breevor had been mistaken.

But he had seen ghosting dark shapes with his own eyes – *hadn't he..?*

He held his breath. He could hear the thumping beat of his own heart in his chest and the rasp of his breath. Then a sound like the *'snick!'* of metal against metal reached his ears. It was muted, and seemed far away. His grip on his M4 carbine tightened and a damp sweat broke out across his brow.

The first North Korean infantry attack came in the middle of the moonless night. It came unannounced; one moment the night was dark and eerily still – and the next it was filled with swarming, running, shooting, shouting shapes that seemed to spring up out of the long grass and surge towards the crest of the hill.

"Open fire!" Hector roared.

Every man in the Company was equipped with the Army's newest night vision goggles, known as the ENVG-B (Enhanced Night Vision Goggle-Binocular). The goggles used augmented reality to clearly identify targets and terrain features in low-light situations. They replaced the typical green monochrome image with white neon outlines and tactical information including compass bearings right in front of the soldier's eyes. Through Hector's ENVG-Bs, the ground along the lower slope seemed to heave with a mass of writhing, charging men.

"Open fire!"

The two M240 machine guns roared into action. Firing from an elevated position that could overwatch the American trenches, the machine guns cut a hammering swathe through the night and lit it with their own fierce, fiery muzzle flashes. Then a Claymore exploded. Its cracking thunder echoed across the sky and Hector saw a bright red flash of flame about two hundred yards to the northeast. Men screamed. M4s added their own throaty roar to the maelstrom of noise and confusion and then a second Claymore exploded to the west.

"Fire!"

The first North Korean infantry appeared from the long grass and came charging up the slope, shooting wildly from the hip and howling a ferocious war cry. The troops from 2nd Platoon opened fire at the running shapes, aiming from close range, all weapons discipline gone to hell in the sudden, savage panic. The Americans blazed and flailed, wasting precious ammunition but pouring enough fire on the rushing North Koreans to crush the momentum of the attack, and then force it back. The North Koreans retreated into the darkness, and as they began to withdraw the two 60mm mortars opened fire on the enemy, their rounds arcing into the night and falling on the lower slopes. The sound of each mortar shell exploding sounded puny compared to the heavy thunder of an artillery round.

Gayle Nordenman had fought from one of the north-facing trenches. He slapped a fresh magazine into his M4 and crawled out of the foxhole, slithering over the rocks until he reached the crest.

"Casualties?" Hector asked his XO.

"None," Nordenman said. "But that won't be the last attack. I think they were just testing our perimeter – probing for a weakness. When they come again, it's going to get ugly, man."

Hector nodded. For all the savage fury of the first enemy attack, he too had noticed how quickly the North Koreans had aborted the assault. Typically, the enemy drove home their charges with mindless, suicidal frenzy. "Concur," he said, then turned to look for his FIST leader.

Lieutenant Jane Parker was crouched in cover behind rocks with the rest of her team, defending their precious radio gear. Hector drew the young, serious-faced woman aside and spoke to her urgently.

"Get the radio link to our arty support open and keep it hot. I don't want to be fucked around for a fire mission when the shit hits the fan, understand?"

Parker nodded. She scurried to her radio. Hector's next task was to inform HQ they were under attack. He called for his senior RTO.

"Contact headquarters and let them know the enemy are attacking our position in Company strength or greater... and see if there is any air support we can call on. There's got to be Apaches somewhere nearby." Hector's mind was a whir, but his training overrode the instinct for panic, giving him a guideline of clear sequential procedures to follow. For his numbed, sleep-deprived brain that training was something he could fall back on, and would ultimately save men's lives. He was about to order a flare launched when the night once again erupted in shouts and heaving movement, and then it was too late to do anything other than fight for their lives.

Because the North Koreans were attacking again.

Chapter 5:

The enemy swarmed forward through the long grass. The element of surprise had been lost and now they came forward in a surging mass of screaming bodies, throwing themselves with suicidal fanaticism at the American trenches.

"Fire!" Hector bellowed and the trench lines erupted in stabbing flames of muzzle flash that painted the night lurid shades of orange.

None of the North Koreans wore body armor.

They died in their droves.

The Americans piled the enemy dead up in front of the trenches creating a bulwark of shattered bodies that the surviving North Koreans had to scramble over. One enemy soldier was shot in the face and thrown back in a gush of blood into the men following him. Another North Korean had his chest flayed open by a hail of M4 fire, spattering guts and gore across the rocks. All along the dark heaving line the enemy troops were mown down, yet still they charged.

A grenade exploded in the long grass and hurled three North Koreans into the air, their bodies shredded by shrapnel. Hector sprinted for the closest trench and opened fire into the night, swinging his M4 onto a North Korean who was emerging from the long grass, his body silhouetted by the flash and roar of grenades exploding and his outline glowing bright white in Hector's NGVs. Hector felt rather than saw the stream of bullets hit the enemy soldier, striking him in the chest and knocking him backwards. The North Korean staggered and dropped his weapon. His hands clutched for his chest and then he fell to the ground, his dark eyes blazing with feral loathing.

The line of enemy soldiers wavered, fell back into the night, and then came again. Quite suddenly, and with a shocking roar of sound, an enemy machine gun howled into hammering life from somewhere on the eastern flank. Hector turned and lifted his head above the eyeline of the trench despite the hiss and flail of gunfire, trying to pinpoint the HMG's location. The machine gun was enfilading the line of American trenches with withering streams of tracer fire, forcing the men to cower for cover.

On the crest of the hill, and behind a palisade of stacked boulders, the two Company mortars were turned and zeroed in on the enemy machine gun position. The first rounds landed long, exploding harmlessly in the night with their distinctive muted *'crump!'* of sound. Four more rounds straddled the enemy position, but still the North Korean machine gun continued to chatter death across the hillside. Finally, a mortar round landed flush on the enemy HMG position, ripping the night apart in a wicked flash of light and flame and killing the gunners.

But the damage had been done. Under the machine gun's withering hail of constant hammering fire, the enemy troops had moved to the rim of the grassy verge unmolested by American counter-fire. Now they sprang to their feet and came swarming out of the darkness.

"Fire!"

Once again the American troops opened fire but despite the tactical advantage of their hi-tech goggles, this time the enemy seemed too numerous to hold back. Hector scrambled from his trench and retreated up the rocky slope as enemy bullets plucked and fizzed at the air about him.

He ducked behind a boulder as bullets ricocheted shards of stone, slashing his cheek open.

"I want fire support right now!" he had to shout at his FIST Lieutenant to make himself heard. He peered back over his shoulder. The night was swarming with dark shapes, lit by the flickering light of American muzzle flashes. The noise, the darkness and the screams of agony had turned the battlefield into a chaos of confusion. "Tell them to pound the northern slope of the hill!"

Jane Parker dived for her radio.

"Godspeed Six, this is Bad Karma Nine, adjust fire, over. Godspeed Six, this is Bad Karma with an adjust fire fire-support mission, over."

The radio crackled for an instant. Parker had to press her ear close to pick up the reply over the maelstrom of rising gunfire that seemed to encircle the crest of the hill.

"Bad Karma Nine, this is Godspeed Six. Adjust fire, out."

Parker transmitted the six-digit MGRS (Military Grid Reference System) coordinate which was echoed by the radio operator of the Paladin Battery that was positioned several miles to the south.

"Battalion-strength enemy infantry in the open supported by heavy weapons. Danger close! Repeat, danger close, over."

The 'danger close' code phrase warned the Paladin Battery that American troops were within six hundred meters of the artillery impact point.

The radio operator on the end of the line repeated the message and ended the transmission.

The Paladin FDC (Fire Direction Center) came on the line a few seconds later to transmit an MTO (Message to Observer) explaining to Parker what ammunition would be used, what gun would fire the spotting rounds and which guns would then fire the mission.

"R, F, DPICM in effect, five rounds, over." The sequence of letters told Parker that Dual Purpose Improved Conventional Munition would be used by the Paladins. She acknowledged the call, cut comms and turned back to Hector. The entire radio exchange had taken less than forty seconds

"The artillery is on its way."

Hector nodded and turned his head to the south as if he might see the flash of red flame from the Paladins opening fire on the distant skyline. He saw nothing behind the drifting banks of smoke, still billowing from the battlefield in the valley. Instead, he heard a far-away rumble, like thunder, and a moment later the air overhead filled with the shriek of an incoming artillery round.

The six M109 Paladin 155mm turreted self-propelled howitzers of Charlie Battery, 113th Field Artillery, 30th Armored Brigade Combat Team were in a field, sixteen kilometers south of 'Little Janice' hill. The artillery unit was based in North Carolina and was nicknamed the 'Old Hickory' brigade in honor of American President Andrew Jackson, due to the original division being composed of National Guard units from areas where he lived. The men who served the Paladins were experienced combat veterans who knew their lethal trade.

The first round from the American howitzers screamed through the night sky and fell into a narrow ravine beyond the northern slope of the hill. Jane Parker watched the round explode in a flash of flames well behind the North Korean troops. Parker snatched up the radio.

"Direction two-one-zero-zero, drop three-zero-zero, left one-five-zero!" Parker called in the adjusted coordinates.

The second round hit the reverse slope of the hill and landed flush amongst the enemy infantry in a crashing eruption that shook the ground beneath her feet.

"Fire for effect, over!"

"Fire for effect, out."

The Paladins of Charlie Battery opened fire.

It sounded like the apocalypse had come to the hillside to engulf the troops of 'Culprit' Company. The howitzers roared and the rounds came crashing down on the slope of the hill in a thunderous fury. One round landed short, destroying a grove of trees right on the lip of an American trench and injuring the two soldiers it contained, but the rest of the massive artillery rounds exploded with lethal accuracy amongst the North Koreans as they were preparing to charge again. Shrapnel cut one enemy soldier in half and turned his remains to bloody mush. Dozens more were immolated by the fearsome explosions. The hillock shook and trembled and the air filled with lethal menace. Dozens more North Koreans were ripped to bloody pieces in the cataclysm of fire and screaming metal.

"Repeat!" Jane Parker crouched behind cover and shouted into the radio as bullets ricocheted off the rocks and the smoke from the artillery rounds drifted up the hill like a rolling bank of fog. Through the haze she could still see hundreds of enemy troops surging towards the crest of the hill, throwing themselves frenetically onto the American guns. The slope was in an uproar of automatic machine gun fire and grenade explosions, and yet through it all the agonized screams of dying men still pierced the clamor. "Repeat! Immediate suppression!"

'Immediate suppression' was the most desperate request an artillery battery could receive. It called for every available gun to fire whatever round and fuse were loaded.

"Repeat. Immediate suppression, out."

The Paladins fired again but now the northern slope of the hill was a wasteland of dead bodies and churned, cratered earth. There was no one left to kill; the wave of enemy troops were already around the crest of 'Little Janice' and threatening to overrun 'Culprit' Company's positions.

Hector, his face cut and bleeding, watched the incoming rounds fall. The explosions lit up the night and silhouetted the enemy troops as they surged forward. He seized Parker's shoulder and the FIST Lieutenant spun round, her face white.

"Tell the arty to drop on our position," Hector made the dire decision.

"Sir?" Parker looked horrified.

"Fucking tell them!" Hector bellowed. It was the only way he could be heard above the maelstrom of the battle. He turned and stared around the rim of the perimeter. Every soldier in the Company was engaging the enemy from close range. The roar of the firefight reached a thunderous frenzy.

"Tell them to drop on our position!" Hector shouted again.

"We'll be killed!" Parker's pale face was horror-stricken.

"We'll be killed if they don't!" Hector retorted. He could read the battle by the sounds of the fighting. The North Koreans were pressing the perimeter on every side. The frantic desperation of the firefight reached a crescendo and he sensed instinctively that the next few minutes would decide their fate. It would take only one more rush of enemy troops for the American trenches to be overrun. Once the enemy were through their lines, the battle would become a savage slaughter. The North Koreans would be merciless in their bloody lust for revenge.

Parker picked up the radio and gave the Paladins coordinates for their position.

"Fire for effect, over. Danger close! Danger close!"

There was a brief delay. Parker hung on the line waiting for the confirmation. Around the crest of the hill the battle continued to roar. A private from 1st Platoon threw himself on an enemy grenade that landed in his trench, killing himself but saving the lives of the three soldiers beside him. Two men fighting on the eastern slope died of gruesome head wounds and were thrown back in the dirt, while all around them others fought on grimly, firing and reloading until their faces were stained with dirt and grime and only their eyes showed white and terrible.

"Fire for effect, out," the artillery radioman confirmed Parker's order.

She threw down the radio and stared up at Hector, appalled at what she had done, the accusation in her eyes dark and malevolent. She had just ordered an entire battery of 155mm howitzers to open fire on them.

"Incoming!" Hector went grimly down the slope, shouting futilely to pass on the warning of imminent danger above the roar of the firefight. His voice was lost in the roar of combat, but as the wave of fresh artillery rounds arced through the sky and began their terminal descent, the Americans in their trenches sensed the monstrous threat. They threw themselves down in their trenches and covered their heads as the first of the Paladin rounds began to tear the crest of the hillside apart.

The first incoming round landed on the eastern side of the slope, smashing the rock-face into a million flying fragments that filled the air with whistling debris. The second round exploded a split-second later, landing on the southern face of the hill in a fireball of flame. Jane Parker and her FIST team fled the hilltop and threw themselves down into the nearest trench. A moment later John Hector dived after them, crashing into the ditch in an awkward tumble of bodies as the remaining rounds of the opening salvo landed.

The fierce explosions tore the northern crest of the hill apart, landing indiscriminately amongst the North Koreans as they emerged from the long grass. One round erupted just twenty feet away from Richard Curry's trench and the force of the explosion lifted the rookie Lieutenant clear off his feet and slammed him back against the far wall of the pit. A tree was uprooted and crashed to the ground, and then the air was thick with dust and debris and billowing clouds of choking smoke as the thunderstorm of shrapnel and explosions thrashed and howled and heaved.

As a child Hector had lived through a twister and now the terror of surviving that tornado revisited him as the artillery barrage raged across the hill. He pressed his face into the dirt and covered his head with his hands. The ground beneath him ruptured and heaved and he was utterly at fate's mercy. He tried to remember snatches of a prayer because to be caught in the eye of an artillery barrage was to be an instant away from a man meeting his maker.

A howitzer round landed somewhere close to where Hector lay and the ground seemed to tear apart around him. Huge clods of earth rained down and pummelled his back, and the air turned red-hot and choking. Dust and dirt filled his mouth and nostrils. He hacked up phlegm and blood, then was gripped by a coughing fit as the air was whipped into a frenzy by the crashing explosion. From behind him he heard someone scream in agony but the shriek was cut short by the crashing detonation of another howitzer round. One of the other men in the trench was sobbing, paralyzed with terror. The man tried to flee the trench, screaming on the edge of suicidal madness. Strong hands wrestled the man back down to the bottom of the pit just as the final artillery round crashed down on the crest of the hill, sending a wall of lethal shrapnel spraying through the air.

The silence in the aftermath of the holocaust was eerie. The Americans rose from their trenches, stunned and bleary-eyed. The crest of the hill was veiled in a thick drifting cloud of smoke and dirt. Hector peered cautiously above the lip of the trench, and blinked. His ears were ringing and everything seemed remote and far away as though viewed through a smeared lens. He spat a mouthful of grit and stared in numbed awe.

Around him the rest of the Company's troops slowly emerged through the haze, moving about the ruined crest of the hill like survivors of a plane crash. They tripped and stumbled, stared blankly and swayed. One man dropped to his knees and wept. Another soldier cried out, "Billy! Oh, fuck!" because his best friend in the Company had been decapitated by flying shrapnel. The sobbing man reeled away from the dismembered corpse, tears of grief streaming down his cheeks.

The North Korean attack had been decimated. The carnage was appalling. The dead lay in piles around the rim of the crest. Most of the bodies had been mauled by shrapnel. They looked like their remains had been savaged by wild animals. Bloodied stumps of limbs, matted chunks of bleeding flesh, and the blue swollen slime of entrails were strewn haphazardly across the rocks, the hacked flesh quietly steaming in the cool night air. The gruesome stench of death coated the back of Hector's throat and invaded his nostrils as he walked dazedly from trench to trench. Every step seemed to reveal some fresh appalling horror. He had never seen the apocalyptic after-effects of an artillery barrage up close before. It was a slaughteryard; the ground stained red with dripping blood.

He stumbled over an arm, severed from its body at the shoulder and recoiled away. Gayle Nordenman loomed out of the smoke and dust. The XO looked like a walking corpse. His face was blanched white with horror. He looked at Hector but there were simply no words. Mercifully the night blanketed the worst of the carnage. In the dawn it would be worse…

"Dead and injured?" Hector's voice sounded hollow in his own ears. A nerve in his right thigh was twitching uncontrollably.

Nordenman licked dry, cracked lips. "Four dead, including Billy Bowen," he said solemnly. "Eight injured. Most with bullet wounds. A couple caught pieces of shrapnel…"

Hector stared down at his boots. They were spattered in blood and gore. "I'm going to have to live with that for the rest of my life," Hector looked like a penitent man, his features twisted with remorse. "I called in the arty. I'm responsible for those men's deaths and injuries."

Nordenman said nothing.

*

The rest of the 9th Battalion moved forward at sunrise and the men of 'Culprit' Company traipsed, weary and exhausted, off the crest of 'Little Janice' to re-join the unit. A battery of MIM-104 Patriot SAM systems took up position on the hillock to oversee the Army's advance and to protect against the threat of North Korean and Chinese air attacks.

Hector made his way to the rear of the Battalion, his feet leaden, teetering with fatigue and exhaustion.

Lieutenant Colonel Benedict Gallman was perched on the rear ramp of a Bradley Fighting Vehicle, sitting with a map spread across his knees, a steaming mug of coffee by his side. He was clean-shaven and smelled of soap. He sensed a figure loom in front of him, blocking his light, and he looked up with sharp irritation, then flinched. For a moment his eyes seemed confused, as though trying to place the features of the haggard wretch before him. He wrinkled his nose in disgust at the putrid stench wafting from the man. Then recognition dawned in his eyes.

"Hector."

"Sir."

"You look like hell, man."

"Nice of you to notice, sir," Hector sneered the last word and laced his tone with scorn. "It's what happens when you spend a whole day fighting and then fight through the night as well. You get spattered in blood and guts and shit, Colonel."

Gallman said nothing. Hector glared at the man and the Colonel broke eye contact. His eyes dropped guiltily to the map while he composed himself. "I understand your men had a hard time of it last night," the Colonel tried to inflect his voice with authority but it came out wrong. Even in his own ears he sounded weak and flustered.

"Yes," Hector said.

"Casualties?"

"Four dead, eight wounded. I had to call artillery support down on us. We were being overrun by a Battalion-strength enemy infantry attack and my men were exhausted because they had fought a major engagement yesterday and then were ordered to a forward position throughout the night."

Gallman flinched as if he had been stung by the accusation in Hector's tone. He looked up into the other man's hard face and his voice turned placating.

"Yes. I argued the point with Brigade," he lied.

"I'm sure you did... sir," Hector's eyes were dead and black. He glared at Gallman with seething hatred and only the tenuous shreds of his ragged discipline prevented him from punching the man in the face.

"Well, it's a day of rest for your men today," Gallman lightened his tone and changed the subject as though he bore wonderful news. "Time to sleep, eat and wash, I reckon. And once the men are settled and comfortable at the rear I'll be around to visit."

"That will cheer the men up, sir," Hector's voice dripped sarcasm.

Hector's brazen insolence was a measure of his exhaustion and bitter frustration. He no longer cared about the consequences, or the peril to his career. Good men had died yesterday, and his loyalty to their memory overrode any personal consequences for his actions. He felt compelled to give the dead a voice.

"Hector, I don't think I like your tone..." Gallman finally bridled. "What are you trying to say?"

"Eat shit, Colonel," John Hector said and walked away.

*

The rest area for 'Culprit' Company was as far away from Battalion HQ as Lieutenant Colonel Gallman could locate it. The site was just a clearing of dirt and mud with a mess tent and a nearby aid station. The surviving soldiers didn't care; they simply threw themselves down on the ground in deathlike attitudes of exhaustion.

They were starving, sleep-deprived, overwrought and despairing. Almost half the Company were dead or wounded. The men that remained were haggard wretches, caked in mud and blood, stinking and unshaven. They reeked of death and sweat and smoke.

A Chaplain came from the direction of the aid station and began to move quietly amongst the men; a tall sandy-haired figure with a kindly face and a gentle voice. He crouched in the dirt beside a young Private and opened his bible. The two men bowed their heads in a silent prayer.

The bodies of those killed in the night fight were carried to trucks and then driven away. The wounded formed a shuffling line at the aid station. Some of the men had to be carried. A Sergeant from 3rd Platoon would most likely lose his leg to the surgeons after a piece of shrapnel had slashed through his thigh. A young Corporal with a wife and two kids waiting for him in Wyoming nursed the bandaged stump of his left hand and sobbed. Three of his fingers had been severed and his wrist cut open by metal fragments. He wept pitifully because he feared he might never be able to hug his kids again. One of the mortar team shuffled ignominiously, his pants stained brown by faeces. He had diarrhea. He bent at the waist and dry heaved, then lost control of his bowels.

Medics came from the tents and began to disperse amongst the rest of the Company, tending to cuts and bruises. One man took off his boots and discovered his feet covered in angry red welts and blisters. His socks were caked stiff with blood.

The mess tent served the entire Battalion. There was a line-up of cleanly uniformed rear echelon troops holding food trays and waiting to be served. They chatted amongst themselves, fresh-faced and smiling. John Hector narrowed his eyes with savage malice.

"Loftham!" he swayed on his feet, reeling with fatigue. "Loftham!"

Buff – Big Ugly Fat Fucker – Loftham lay on the far side of the rest area. He rolled onto his side and sat up with a groan. "Sir?"

A medic was patching up a cut on the villainous-looking Corporal's knee, strapping the wound with a bandage.

"Are you going to die from your wound?" Hector shouted across the clearing.

"No, sir."

"Then come with me."

The two men strode purposefully towards the mess tent. The REMFs waiting in line saw the pair of soldiers approaching and reeled away from the stench and the murderous gleam in their eyes. The Captain and the Corporal looked like blood-spattered savages.

Hector pushed to the front of the line and Buff Loftham stood at his shoulder with his huge fists bunched like hammers, glaring around the tent.

Hector found the Lieutenant in charge of the mess tent and drew him aside to a quiet corner, well out of earshot.

"Lieutenant, the men in that clearing are troops from 'Culprit' Company. You've heard of us, right? You've heard that we're trouble-makers, that we're the scum of the earth, right?"

The young Lieutenant nodded. His face was white with alarm. Hector had his arm around the man's shoulder, pulling him menacingly close so that the putrid reek of his blood-spattered unwashed and gore-smeared body made the Lieutenant's eyes water.

"Well, those men have just come off the line after twenty-four hours of non-stop fighting," Hector kept his voice calm and measured, and somehow that made his words more menacing than if he had shouted. "They've seen some of their best friends killed, and they've seen men maimed so horribly it would make you puke. They've fought in blood and mud since dawn yesterday. They haven't had a decent meal in all that time. They've had to shit and piss where they stood because the enemy were attacking them and they needed to keep fighting or be killed. Do you understand?"

"Yes, sir."

"Now they're off the line and resting, and all they want is a decent hot meal. Do you think those heroes who were fighting for freedom deserve a meal, Lieutenant?"

"Yes, sir."

"Can you arrange to have food brought to them, Lieutenant? They're exhausted. They're wounded. They can't line up; they can barely stand."

"I'll... I'll see to it immediately, sir."

Hector smiled thinly.

Most of the men slept through the afternoon while the Company's Sergeants and Gayle Nordenman sought ammunition, replaced faulty gear, and filled in the inevitable casualty reports and after-action reports. A dozen replacement troops were brought into the Company, straight off the transport planes from the States. They arrived in clean uniforms and with fresh faces into a world of haggard horror. The veterans of 'Culprit' Company scavenged their rucks for cigarettes, clean socks and underwear. It was callous welcome to the war in Asia.

Hector met the new recruits and spoke to them briefly, then left them to Nordenman to distribute throughout the Company's depleted ranks.

At sunset the Lieutenant Colonel's M-ATV came splashing through the mud and parked by the aid station. Gallman stepped down from the vehicle and struck an arrogant imperious gesture, reminiscent of his idol, General Patton. He surveyed the rest area, saw the tall figure of Captain Hector, and strode purposefully in the opposite direction surrounded by a cluster of functionaries. He stopped to chat briefly with men who were woken from their sleep by the Colonel's staff for a handshake. It was like a slick politician's whistle-stop tour during an election. A grim smile, a few quick meaningless words and then he fled back to his headquarters.

*

"Listen up," Hector drew his command team around him, his face as bleak as a funeral director in the dusk light. "I've just come from a briefing. It's on. It's happening tomorrow at dawn. The Army is starting the assault against Kaesong. Our first objective is the massive industrial area to the south of the city. We roll out at 0400. Trucks will take us to the assembly point." He paused for a moment to judge the reaction of the men around him. As he expected, they were downcast but stoic and tight-lipped. Hector went on.

"Our Company objective is a machinery parts factory to the west of the main arterial road," he showed them a satellite image of the general area and pointed to the building that 'Culprit' Company had been tasked to seize. The two-story building was set in a clearing of space beside a four lane stretch of highway that hooked like a reversed letter 'J' through the heart of the sprawling complex of factories, warehouses and worker apartment blocks.

"Intel says this attack is going to be a motherfucker," Hector told them straight. "The North Koreans are apparently being supported by units of Chinese infantry and have fortified the roads into the area, and probably the buildings. They're going to be dug in deeper than an Alabama tick. We have to burrow the fuckers out."

"Is it just our Company attacking, Captain?" young Richard Curry asked earnestly.

"No," Hector said. "This time we attack as a Battalion. Bravo and Delta Companies will be on our flanks, but they each have their own objectives. There will be mech infantry involved in the advance as well, but their focus will be the eastern areas of the complex."

"Tanks?"

"Once we secure our objectives the Abrams will push forward and secure the road that runs north to Kaesong City. But until we can break down the enemy's defenses and take out their anti-tank emplacements and RPG teams, we're on our own."

"Artillery?"

"Shit loads of it," Hector said. "It begins at dawn tomorrow morning… and the Air Force is apparently going to fly bombing missions – if they can get their pampered darling pilots out of their comfortable air-conditioned barracks in time…"

There was a ripple of grudging resentment from the gathered men, typical of the rivalry between branches of the armed forces. Hector noted with a wry smile that nothing banded the men together faster than mentioning the comparatively luxurious war the Air Force were so far apparently enjoying.

"But for all that's been promised in support of the attack, we know it's our job to do the dirty work," Hector added a final caution. "So, make sure your men are briefed and keep them informed throughout the night. Supply trucks, stores, and ration trucks will be marshaled and waiting for us at the assembly point. Let's be sure our guys have plenty of everything they need before we go back into battle. This fight could take an hour, or we could get snared into another Stalingrad-like siege that drags on for a week. Make sure the men are fully equipped and that they have all the ammunition and water they can carry. Hooah?"

"Hooah!"

The 'Culprits' were going back to war.

Chapter 6:

The men of 9th Battalion stood in a dirt clearing as the first hint of the new dawning day lit the distant skyline. The troops were dull silhouettes in the gloom, assembled around a fleet of waiting transport trucks as Lieutenant Colonel Gallman lifted his voice to address them.

To the side, and well away from the troops, two news camera crews were filming the preparations for the imminent attack for broadcast back in America. Gallman sensed he had an audience and he strutted and preened from the back of a truck, making a speech that the troops listened to with dull eyes.

Hector let the words drift over him and instead watched the transport crews prepping the trucks that would take them to the staging point for the attack.

Gallman's speech ended with a whimpered, "Hooah," and then mute silence.

The troops drifted towards the trucks that were warming up in the brittle chill air, belching diesel exhaust in great black clouds of smog.

"Okay, 'Culprits' take a knee you god-forsaken bastards," Hector raised his voice and the Company gathered around him.

He took a long moment to study their faces in the strengthening light. The men stared back at him. They were dirty, filthy wretches, unshaven and haggard. The strain of constant combat was in their faces and in their haunted eyes. In the distance, an artillery battery somewhere to the south of the clearing opened fire. The sounds of the huge guns firing seemed to punctuate his words. Hector looked around him and with a sickening shock realized how few of the Company remained. Seeing the men assembled like this was the first visual representation of how savagely their ranks had been depleted by endless fighting. The Company was barely at half strength.

"We were never any good," he walked a small circuit in the dirt. "We were always the troublemakers, the misfits… the damned," he told them. "We've fought this fucking war for weeks on end, knee deep in guts and blood and gore, and there's another fight coming now. It's there," he pointed north. "And the enemy are waiting for us. We all know what today is going to bring. Tonight, when the fighting is done, some of us won't be alive anymore."

He paused to let that reality sink home. He saw men turn solemnly to the guys beside them as if trying to burn their features into their memories.

"But if I'm going into another fight, I want it to be with you guys," Hector lifted his voice and met each man's gaze. "I want to fight shoulder-to-shoulder with real men, real soldiers – and that's who you are. You're rough, you're tough, you're the meanest bastards in this fucking Army. I'm proud of you," his voice caught with an unexpected swell of emotion. "Each and every one of you is a god-damned hero."

Hector's words were brusquely choked off by a spontaneous wild cheer. Even the transport troops waiting in their trucks joined the swelling chorus of shouts. Sergeant Breevor bellowed, "Who are we?" and the Company to a man shouted back, "The Culprits! Hooah!"

The troops piled into the waiting trucks brimming with energy, buzzing and slapping each other on the back. They were motivated and inspired. The lorries drove them forward to the pre-assault position just a mile south of the Kaesong Industrial Estate.

The world was lightening quickly. The dawning day revealed a clear blue sky above a horizon still smudged with smoke.

The trucks parked in a dense grove of trees beside a network of dirt tracks that all lead north. 'Culprit' Company clambered out of the vehicles and Hector went to find someone in command. When he came back, Gayle Nordenman and Ethan Breevor were waiting for him. The Company were concealed in the trees, the men smoking, or trying to feign casual indifference. Some men slept fitfully.

"What are we up against?" Nordenman asked. He looked thin and pale, as though the constant strain had whittled him down in size.

Hector glanced at his watch. "The artillery barrage starts in a few minutes," he said. "We advance at 0700." He produced a marked map and showed it to his XO and First Sergeant. "Bravo Company are half a click to our west. Delta Company are to our east. We move forward at 0645 to this trail," he pointed to a wriggling pale line on the map. "That's our launch point for the attack."

Breevor and Nordenman studied the map carefully. From the trail they would need to cross a half-mile of open ground before they intersected the main road into the industrial complex and encountered the first buildings. Neither man looked pleased.

"Smoke?"

"At the end of the arty barrage," Hector confirmed. As if the Gods had heard his voice, at that moment the ground rumbled and the distant horizon was lit by a fiery glow of red light that seemed to rim the edge of the world. Three seconds later the first artillery rounds shrieked overhead and landed somewhere beyond sight to the north. The thunder of the explosions carried in waves to where they stood, followed by black boiling smoke that seemed to spread across the northern skyline like a looming thunderstorm.

"It's started," Breevor grunted.

For an unrelenting hour the massed guns of the Allies hammered the Kaesong Industrial estate region with a mixture of white phosphorus and high-explosive heavy artillery rounds. The artillery tactic was called a 'shake and bake' and was designed to drive the enemy troops from their cover. High overhead South Korean and American fighter-bombers dropped JDAMs on key enemy installations. The sky turned eerily dark and the sun rose red like a ball of fire behind the thick pall of smoke.

It had been the way of war for a millennium; an artillery attack to soften the enemy and shatter their defensive positions followed by a massed infantry assault to overwhelm the shell-shocked defenders. The advent of the tank and attack aircraft had done nothing to revolutionize war. For all the technology attached to the weapons industry, the art of warfare had changed little in a thousand years. Ultimately men on the ground must die for a chance to triumph.

Missiles streaked across the sky and the booming roar of jet fighters on afterburner competed with the thunder of the pounding guns until the clamor was a cacophony of unrelenting violent noise. North Korean SAM missiles chased the Allied fighter jets across the heavens. An American F-18 was clipped on the wing by an enemy surface-to-air missile and went tumbling across the smoke-drenched sky to its fiery doom. Then a flight of four lethal A-10 Warthogs swept in low from the west. Hector saw them following the contours of the undulating ground as they burst through the smoke at low altitude, targeting enemy anti-tank emplacements. The blunt snouts of the Warthogs erupted in leaping flames and a shroud of grey smoke as their massive autocannons went to work. One of the A-10's jinked and then faltered. The aircraft dipped below the rise of a distant hill and two seconds later a flaming explosion lit the sky. Another A-10 reeled away from the fight streaming black smoke. The aircraft limped south on a course that carried it directly over the grove of trees where 'Culprit' Company was waiting anxiously for their attack orders.

Hector watched the A-10 as it flashed overhead, slowly sinking down the sky in the final stages of its death throes.

A Humvee skidded to an urgent halt and a junior officer from HQ bundled out of the side door of the vehicle. He was red-faced and sweating. He found Hector on the edge of the tree line.

"Captain, orders from Battalion. You're to move immediately up to your launch position."

Hector looked for Nordenman and Breevor. The Sergeant began bellowing orders. Suddenly the waiting was over and now the fighting was imminent. A new energy infected the men; fear, anxiety and trepidation swept through the group.

They gathered up their kit and gave their weapons a final inspection, their voices hushed but infected with angst.

There was no false bravado.

There were no eager faces.

Each veteran knew all-too-well the terror of combat.

The 'Culprits' marched with stoic resolve into the gaping jaws of death.

*

The Company reached the crest of a gentle hill and stared ahead at the Kaesong Industrial region. It was a flat low-rise sprawl of massive factories, worker apartment complexes, and streets lined with warehouses. It was drab, grey and burning. The entire valley was shrouded in smoke. Hector followed the wide grey highway towards the heart of the complex but his view was blotted out by haze and leaping flames. Several of the warehouses to the east of his position had been levelled to debris by the artillery and air attacks. Here and there pockets of ground were blackened scorched ruins. But in other places factory buildings stood, seemingly untouched.

The American soldiers came off the crest and sank down into the long grass. They were barely half a mile from the closest buildings.

Hector looked to his left and right and saw the men of Delta and Bravo Companies also moving up into their attack positions. Hector glanced at his watch.

The artillery barrage suddenly stopped and the world turned ominously eerie. Hector pressed a pair of binoculars to his eyes and tried to locate the factory that was the Company's objective. His eyes found the grey ribbon of highway that cut through the heart of the complex and he followed it, peering through drifting skeins of smoke and leaping tongues of flame until at last his gaze settled on a massive dark grey iron roof. The factory had been hit by artillery fire. Hector could see great holes punched in the building, and a part of a collapsed brick wall. The rest of the factory was shrouded in a bank of grey drifting smoke.

He felt a sick lurch of foreboding. Between where he stood and his objective was a wide-open clearing and a four lane stretch of highway, lined on both sides by small buildings and several apartment complexes. It was a mile and a half long suicidal obstacle course with death and danger lurking around every blind corner. He handed the binoculars to Sergeant Breevor.

Then the artillery opened fire again after a respite of less than a minute. More shells arced through the air, whistling as they made their terminal descent. They blew apart with a muted *'crump!'* amidst the outskirts of the industrial region.

"Smoke," Ethan Breevor said. It was the last phase of the pre-attack plan. Hector felt his stomach tie itself in knots. Behind the line of infantry, Abrams tanks, Bradleys and Strykers were forming up. The mech infantry aboard the Bradleys and Strykers were preparing to dash east to assault the far flank of the complex. The Abrams tanks were waiting for the infantry to clear the highways of enemy anti-tank positions. Once the route through the heart of the industrial sprawl was cleared, they would charge forward to secure the road that ran north to the city of Kaesong itself.

The smoke continued to thicken, round after round falling on the edge of the North Korean industrial estate. Then Hector's RTO gripped his shoulder.

"HQ on the line, Capt'n. They want us to start the attack."

Hector nodded. His mouth was dry; his eyes burned from the smoke, and his ears rang with the echo of the artillery barrage.

He got to his feet and punched the air with his clenched fist. His legs felt weak. His throat felt like it was lined with shards of broken glass. "'Culprit' Company! Go! Go! Go!"

*

The Company moved forward in a wedge with 3rd Platoon taking the point and 1st and 2nd Platoons supporting on either flank. In the middle of the wedge Hector and Nordenman advanced with the FIST team and the heavy weapons team, both men's eyes anxiously scanning the approaching buildings on the outskirts of the industrial complex. The Company reached the highway without coming under enemy fire.

Allied artillery rounds began falling again, targeting buildings and installations on the northern edge of the complex. The vibrations of each explosion rumbled up through the ground and added to the chaos of noise and smoke the 'Culprits' were advancing warily into. Then – unexpectedly from behind them – they heard the bellow of revving engines and the clatter of steel grinding tracks. Hector turned in dismay and saw a column of Bradley IFVs rumbling down the highway, streaming a tail of dust and dirt in their wake. The Brads were travelling at high speed with a handful of Abrams tanks on their flank, the huge MBTs jouncing and bucking over the uneven terrain as they closed on the nearest buildings.

Hector watched the Brads in astonishment. He turned to Nordenman. "What the fuck is going on? Where did the armor come from?"

The XO shrugged his shoulders and looked perplexed. It was yet another element to add to the chaos of combat – but maybe it was also an opportunity…

The Brads were M2s, designed for recon and troop transport. Each vehicle had a driver, a commander and a gunner, and could carry half a dozen fully equipped soldiers. The vehicles were equipped with an M242 25mm autocannon and an M240C 7.62mm coax machine gun. Hector could see men in the turrets of the lead vehicles, traversing their guns in search for targets.

Hector punched his RTO in the arm. "Find out who those boys are and get 'em on the radio!" he demanded.

The Brads were on the charge. Hector pulled his Company off the highway as the vehicles raced towards them. On the flank of the advancing vehicles, the lead Abrams suddenly opened fire, the muzzle-flash of its 120mm gun spitting a huge tongue of flame. Hector turned his head and saw a building on the outskirts of the complex erupt in a ball of flames and debris. A moment later a ribbon of grey smoke streaked across the sky. The RPG had been fired from the second-story window of a small building close to the highway. The missile struck the lead Bradley a glancing blow and deflected away. The Brad shuddered on its tracks and slewed to the shoulder of the road. A few seconds later the gunner behind the Bushmaster opened fire, thrashing the building where the RPG had been fired from with a torrent of roaring lead.

"Things are about to kick off," Nordenman observed laconically.

"No shit!" Hector crouched low to the ground with one hand clamping his helmet tight to his head. The Company were caught between the advancing armor and the outskirts of the industrial complex, trapped in a sudden crossfire of missiles and machine guns.

Hector's RTO tugged on the sleeve of his jacket to get his attention. "The Brads are A Company, 3rd Battalion, 66th AR Regiment."

"What the fuck are they doing here?"

"Their breach into the city on the eastern flank has been closed by IEDs and heavy anti-tank fire. Lots of casualties and chaos. The Brads and Abrams were sent west to find a new route into the city."

Hector nodded grimly. The attack to the east had already turned into an epic clusterfuck, and the assault was just a few minutes old. So much for artillery and air support pulverising the enemy before the attack, Hector thought bitterly, then shrugged off the news. The setback to the east was someone else's problem. He had his own hell to deal with. He got to his feet and dashed forward to where 3rd Platoon were laying in the dirt covering the advance. The Platoon leader had been killed in combat the previous day. Hector found the Sergeant leading the men and shouted in his ear as the column of Brads began to race past them.

"Get your men up and get them following the Brads along the highway!" Hector had to shout to make himself heard. The Brads raced past in a billow of flying dust and debris and roaring noise. "We'll use them to cover our advance. Move it!"

The Company leaped to its feet and began a helter-skelter charge towards the outskirts of the city, trailing the column of Bradleys, running into a wall of dust and smoke and noise.

The lead elements of the armored column ran headlong into stiff North Korean resistance. Hector heard a thunderous explosion followed a few seconds later by a second loud roar of noise. Suddenly the highway ahead was blocked by the mangled wreckage of two Brads. Both vehicles were burning infernos beneath tall black columns of smoke. Gunfire erupted to the Company's right and the 'Culprits' broke into their separate platoons and scattered for cover. On the highway, the backed-up convoy of Bradleys had ground to a halt. Ramps dropped and mech infantry spilled from the vehicles, scattering left and right as they exited. From surrounding windows enemy machine guns opened fire. The mech infantry used the cluster of vehicles around them as temporary cover but were in danger of becoming pinned down. North Korean machine guns firing from elevated windows further along the highway cut a swathe through the milling chaos. Hector saw two men spill out of the darkened gloom of their Brad into the morning light, their guns at their shoulders, fear and tension tight in their faces as they cleared the ramp and then dashed to the right. They ran straight into a fusillade of enemy machine gun fire. Both men went down in a bleeding, screaming mess. The closest man had been shot in the face. He lay on the blacktop, his arms flung wide, his legs drumming against the ground with half his head missing. The second man had taken two rounds in the hip. He screwed up his face in screaming agony and slumped against the side of the dust-coated Bradley. He dropped his weapon and clutched desperately at the searing pain. He slid down the vehicle, leaving a smear of bright red blood and lay on the road with his legs in front of him and slowly dying.

Hector tore his eyes away from the dying soldier and focussed his attention on the stretch of highway ahead of him. It was four lanes of blacktop barricaded by blazing Brads and surrounded on their side by two and three-story drab brick buildings, each one streaked with a black coat of pollution and grime. The North Koreans were in those buildings in fortified firing positions and it was 'Culprit' Company's task to fight their way through, and then to mount an attack on their objective factory that lay another mile further along the road. Hector gritted his teeth and took a heartbeat to understand the hell he had been thrown in to.

Everywhere he looked he saw buildings ablaze and tangled rubble. The smoke lay heavy against the ground in dense roiling layers. Floating in the smoke haze were thousands of small burning embers, and along the ground lay spatters and rivulets of white burning phosphorus. The outskirts of the complex had been turned into a holocaust of rubble, twisted metal and burning vehicles. Hector's men were to the right of the road and coming under fire from enemy troops in buildings on the edge of the complex. Somewhere far to his left he heard the thundering roar of an Abrams firing, adding their clamor to the frantic chaos.

Hector was about to order 3rd Platoon forward to assault the closest building when the ripping hammer of a bushmaster chain gun suddenly roared. The gunners in the surviving Bradleys had recovered from the initial enemy onslaught and had opened fire on several buildings on the edge of the highway, prepping the closest buildings for their infantry to storm. Tracer streaked across the sky, tearing chunks from brick walls and disappearing through windows. The North Koreans counterfired. Two RPG rockets flashed through the air on wavering white tails of smoke. One exploded right beside a Bradley, heaving the vehicle up on its suspension, rocking it violently and spattering the steel hull with shrapnel. The other rocket streaked past the side of a vehicle, missing it by less than a meter and exploded harmlessly by the side of the road. The bushmasters turned on the North Koreans with a vengeful fury, smothering the two windows from where the rockets had been launched, demolishing the wall and killing the enemy soldiers inside.

Hector scanned the ground ahead of 'Culprit' Company. There were three squat buildings to their front, connected by a high wire fence to the buildings that lined the highway. His assault plan had already gone to hell. He should be where the mech infantry were; storming down the highway and clearing buildings along the route as they advanced. His only plan now was to get into the fight as quickly as possible to relieve the fury of fire the Bradleys were coming under.

He sprang to his feet and waved the Company forward. The men around him rose, firing as they advanced, peppering the façade of the three buildings ahead of them. The Company's 60mm mortars set up in the shallow depression of a bomb crater and lobbed mortar rounds onto the buildings, getting hits immediately. One of the roofs collapsed in a shower of sparks and flame and dust. Then the two M240B/L machine guns joined the fight. Nordenman had set them up on the edge of the highway, so they could suppress the enemy from the flank without firing through their own advancing men. The machine guns rattled to life and cut a swathe through the smoke swirling air.

"Go hard and fast!" Hector shouted as he dashed forward, urging his men on. They were within a hundred yards of the closest house when suddenly the building ahead of them erupted in flickering muzzle flashes and a bank of smoke. The first North Korean fusillade flew high and wide. Hector heard the bullets rattle and fizz through the air all around him. He doubled over to make himself a smaller target and clenched his teeth, tensing himself for the inevitable pain of a bullet wound. His mind was completely blank; his whole attention focussed on the ground ahead as the buildings drew closer and the men around him began to fall and cry out in bloody agony. A Corporal was hit in the shoulder and spun round like a top, dropping his M4 and clutching at the pain. His face wrenched into a rictus of agony, and he cried out, his voice a shrill kind of scream. He sagged to his knees, his arm awash with blood. Two more men went down, punched off their feet by close-range hits. A man from 3rd Platoon took a hit high up on the thigh but kept running. Momentum carried him three more steps before his leg collapsed beneath him and he stumbled to the dirt.

The machine guns on the flank of the attack turned their aim onto the windows of the buildings, suppressing the North Koreans as the 'Culprits' scrambled to close the distance. Suddenly the building before them blew outwards in a massive explosion that flung cement slabs and roof beams and broken bricks cartwheeling a hundred feet into the air. Debris from the monstrous explosion rained down on the advancing American soldiers, and they covered their heads reflexively and ducked for shelter. An Abrams tank emerged through the smoke, veering across the highway, its steel tracks churning up the blacktop. It plunged down into the dirt and swerved across the path of the advancing soldiers, throwing up a dense bank of dirt and dust. The Abrams turned sharply and ploughed forward like a battering ram, the coax gun slaved to the turret spitting venom. The tank burst through the wire fence and bulldozed through the front wall of the building ahead of it, crushing two enemy soldiers under its massive weight.

"Follow the Abrams!" Hector waved his arms frantically.

The tank was their way through the outskirts of the city.

Chapter 7:

The Abrams stalled amidst the debris and rubble for a moment, its massive engine bellowing as the tank's turret turned towards a small factory several hundred yards ahead. In its wake swarmed the 'Culprits' of 3rd Platoon with Hector leading the way. Lieutenant Curry's 2nd Platoon scattered into the rubble of the destroyed buildings, taking cover and firing to support the advance.

A storm of North Korean gunfire erupted from behind a high brick perimeter wall that cordoned off a complex of single-story warehouses directly ahead of the advance. Hector ducked for cover as the air filled with bullets flying thick as wind-driven rain.

"Jesus!" he gasped, his breathing ragged. He tried to tuck himself into a ball. An enemy machine gun punched a line of bullet holes into a jagged cement slab just inches above his head. Shards of debris and dust filled the air. Hector heard a groan and turned to see a man clutching his shoulder, blood flowing bright red between his fingers. The soldier's face was pale, his expression bewildered until the pain crashed over him in waves and he cried out and dropped to the ground. The Platoon was pinned down and coming under heavy fire. A salvo of RPG rockets sliced through the bullet-torn smoke. One struck the Abrams flush on the turret leaving a black scorch mark. Another struck the tank front on. Both rockets had been fired from a range of just a few hundred yards, but neither had the killing power to penetrate the Abram's armor. For a long moment the tank was shrouded in a veil of black smoke. When the haze cleared, the Abrams began to advance again. Its 120mm gun fired, the recoil rocking the huge steel beast on its suspension as the leaping muzzle-flash lit up the sky. The wall the enemy troops were hidden behind blew apart. The impact of the HE round tore a fifteen-foot-wide breach in the perimeter, hurling chunks of stone and concrete high into the air. Another RPG rocket ripped through the smoke screen, this one fired from an adjoining street off to the Company's right. The rocket had been fired from long range.

It plunged down out of the sky at the end of its arced flight and landed in front of the Abrams, flinging more debris and dust into the air but doing no damage to the advancing tank.

Hector poked his head above the debris that sheltered him and knew the 'Culprits' had to keep advancing into the maelstrom of death and destruction. The enemy were still firing from the wall, pouring down a hailstorm of lead to keep the Company pinned behind cover. Away to his right he could see Lieutenant Curry's men laying prone in the debris and firing downrange at the wall while RPG rockets and enemy gunfire thrashed and roared around them.

Hector snatched for his radio and ordered the mortars to fire smoke ahead of the enemy's defensive position then had the Company's HMGs redeployed to 2nd Platoon. It took two long hellish minutes before the machine guns were in place and the mortars targeted.

The first smoke rounds leaped from the mouths of the 60mm mortars and landed with muted *'crumps!'* fifty yards ahead of the wall the North Korean troops were defending. Two more rounds fell, creeping in increments closer to the wall, the thick white veil quickly blotting out Hector's view. He called in more mortar fire and then waited, counting down sixty long seconds on his wristwatch, playing a game of bluff and counter-bluff.

He knew that as soon as the smoke had begun to blanket the enemy's view, the North Koreans would anticipate an immediate attack. Their rate of fire increased, shooting blindly into the smoke, anticipating hits on the Americans they imagined were charging towards them. Hector let the fusillade flail and thrash the air overhead until he felt the volume of enemy fire begin to wither.

He knew it was now or never.

He sprang to his feet, scrambling across the rubble-strewn ground, and there was a wild frenzied cry in his throat; an incoherent sound of rage and fear and terror and fury. The men from 3rd Platoon saw their Captain suddenly lurch into the open and they broke cover, running with him, the same strangled cry of raw terror and fighting madness in their voices.

There was three hundred yards of tangled debris and destroyed buildings between the 'Culprits' and the wall being defended by the enemy. The Abrams surged forward with the infantry in its shadow. The tank's main gun fired again and smashed another great chunk from the wall. The range was so close and the impact of the explosion so fierce that chunks of brick and slabs of concrete rained down on the advancing Americans.

Hector ran through the haze with his lungs on fire and his body a lather of sweat. The stench of death and the fumes from the smoke caught in his throat. He could see through the veil of crashing thunderous confusion that several warehouse buildings beyond the wall were ablaze. He jinked left as a flurry of enemy bullets twitched the smoke, then fired his M4 from the hip. A man next to him tripped over a tangle of barbed wire and went stumbling to the ground, cursing. Another soldier took an enemy bullet flush in the chest and staggered backwards. His body armor saved his life. He sucked in a deep wheezing breath and lumbered on, the men around him plucking at his elbow to keep him on his feet and moving forward.

A knot of men sheltering in the shadow of the advancing Abrams were thrown to the ground when an RPG rocket suddenly streaked through the smoke haze and exploded against the tank's heavy side armor. Two of the soldiers were killed in the explosion, their bodies ripped to shreds by flailing shrapnel. Another man had his head sliced open. He clutched at his face, trying to cram his eyes back into their sockets as a torrent of spattered spraying blood splashed the dirt. The man staggered in a small circle, moaning in gasping horror until an enemy bullet struck him in the back and punched him dead to the ground.

Hector ran on.

Behind 3rd Platoon followed the men of 1st Platoon, the two units merging together as they closed on the wall. The North

Koreans defended resolutely, firing in clusters so the sound of gunfire came like a rolling crescendo of noise, rippling along the line behind a thick bank of roiling smoke. A couple of Americans threw grenades while on the run, but most of the men simply put their heads down and drove forward, cringing with the expectation of death at every step. Some of the men muttered prayers as they charged into the waiting guns. Some men sobbed, fighting to overcome their fear. Others cowered behind cover, their faces ashen and stricken with terror.

On the flank of the attack Richard Curry was calmly directing 2nd Platoon's fire, coaching the machine gunners from the heavy weapons squad and pointing out enemy targets like a battle-hardened veteran. He saw a group of enemy soldiers behind a swirl of smoke. They were running through the rubble to take up new firing positions behind a corner of the high wall. Curry tracked their movement until they momentarily disappeared and slapped the machine gunner in front of him on his helmet with the flat of his hand.

"Right fifteen degrees," Curry shouted. "A handful of 'crazies' looking to enfilade the attack. Cut the bastards down!"

The gunner took a moment to adjust his aim and peered down the weapon's sights. He saw enemy soldiers reveal themselves, their weapons raised. As they opened fire on the Americans charging towards them, the M240B/L roared to life.

The section of high wall dissolved into a dust storm of flying concrete chunks as the machine gun roared. The North Koreans went down in untidy crumpled bundles under the withering squall of fire. Curry patted the gunner on the back and squinted his eyes. He could see John Hector in the chaos of rubble, leading the charge to reach the wall. Incredibly the Captain was still alive; still driving forward into the enemy's hellish crossfire.

Hector reached the wall at last and flattened his back against a cold slab of concrete. His face was a mask of spattered blood and mud, streaked with rivulets of sweat. His eyes were red-raw, his heart pounding furiously within the cage of his ribs. He stared back across the wasteland he had crossed, aghast at the trail of carnage that had been left in his wake. There were dead American bodies amongst the ruins and the rubble – his men. He saw a corpse crumpled over a twisted length of steel girder. The back of the man's head was a bloody mush. Beside the body was another soldier, laying in the dirt, his arms flung wide and his head twisted so that his lifeless eyes were turned to Hector. There were others too. Some had been ripped apart by shrapnel, others had been shot. Some were wounded, dragging themselves through the rubble, shattered legs trailing blood streaks behind them as they crawled, sobbing in agony, through a holocaustic landscape of smoke and fire and devastation.

Through the swirling banks of smoke more running men emerged, joining Hector in the shelter of the wall. The North Korean fire had thinned and become sporadic. Hector edged his way towards one of the breaches the Abrams had ripped into the wall and lobbed a grenade through the opening.

"Go!" he shouted and led the advance into the courtyard of the factory complex. The wall encircled a maze of small industrial buildings and sheds clustered around an aircraft hangar. Many of the smaller buildings were on fire, their roofs collapsed. Mountains of grey rubble from bomb-damaged walls lay scattered across the ground. Amidst the ruins were dozens of dead North Koreans.

Hector cleared the breach in the wall and dropped to his knee, M4 pressed to his shoulder, his eye following the direction of the weapon's barrel as he scanned quickly for enemy targets. A bullet smacked into the concrete just a few inches from his head. Hector flinched instinctively and then saw a wisp of smoke drifting away from the window of a building a hundred yards to his left. He scrambled for cover behind a chunk of broken concrete as the men following him surged forward to establish a perimeter. Hector scanned the window and a moment later saw a head appear. He fired instantly and the enemy soldier was thrown back out of sight.

Ethan Breevor was one of the men who surged through the breach. He dropped to the ground beside Hector and pulled his weapon to his shoulder. "The fuckers don't know when they're beaten," the Sergeant said.

Hector grunted. He saw a flicker of movement from another window in the same building he had just fired on and he narrowed his eyes. "What kind of shape are we in?"

"We're in a shit state," Breevor said bluntly. The men pouring through the breach in the wall were scattering forward, each taking up prone firing positions in the rubble. "Haggarty is dead. Shrapnel. And a handful of the new recruits are already dead or wounded."

"They don't last long," Hector muttered. "This war is a fucking meat grinder." The shadowy shape appeared again in the window and this time Hector fired instinctively. The magazine clicked empty and with a few quick deft movements Hector reloaded.

"One of the FNGs was from your hometown," Breevor mentioned. "He reckons he knew your kid brother. He took a bullet in the chest, the poor bastard. Somehow it missed his body armor. I stayed with him until the medics arrived, but he ain't gonna make it."

The last of the 1st and 3rd Platoon survivors cleared the breach and scattered for cover. The battlefield had turned eerily quiet. An ominous pall of stillness hung in the air, like the moments before a thunderstorm breaks. Beyond the walls of the complex the larger battle still raged, punctuated by explosions and screams and chattering automatic weapons fire – but here it was deathly quiet. The looming silence made the hairs at the back of Hector's neck stand on end.

He was about to reach for his radio when suddenly a distant bugle sounded. Hector frowned. The noise of trilling notes was so incongruous that it seemed almost comically out of place on a modern battlefield. He stole a stricken glance sideways at Breevor. "That sounds like trouble."

No sooner had he uttered the words than a swarm of North Korean infantry appeared from the warren of narrow laneways between the factory buildings. They came as a screaming maniacal horde, hatred and fanaticism in their eyes, firing their weapons on the run as they burst into the open.

Two men from 1st Platoon who had taken cover forward of the rest of the Company had time only to fire off a panicked flurry of bullets before they were overwhelmed by the surging enemy who attacked them in a frenzy of bare hands and bayonets.

"Fire!" Hector shouted the order. It was too late to save the two men. They were torn to pieces by the horde and trampled to pulp. But the rest of 1st and 3rd Platoon's guns opened fire. The hail of bullets slashed and decimated the charging North Koreans but still the enemy surged forward a triumphant roar in their throats as they threw themselves at the Americans. The front row of North Koreans fell, their bodies thrown back in bloody shreds by concentrated aimed fire. One enemy soldier was shot three times in the chest, and he fell in a shattered mess to the ground. Another man staggered, his face a bloody mask from a bullet wound. He sagged to his knees and was knocked over and trampled by the men following.

Hector fired at a North Korean Captain who was at the forefront of the swarming horde. The man's uniform was tattered and streaked with dirt, his face terrible with his fury. His head was swathed in grubby bandages. Hector's bullets caught the enemy officer in the throat and the man fell, gasping and clutching at the wound.

For a moment the battle stalled. The charging North Koreans swerved away from the fury of American fire and burrowed into cover. Some enemy soldiers dropped behind debris and began to return fire. Others battered down locked doors or threw themselves through windows to escape the fusillade. Ethan Breevor pressed his sweaty blood-spattered face close to Hector's. "You've got two choices, sir," he spoke quickly, reading the tempo of the battle and understanding that the next few seconds might determine its outcome. "We can either attack or fall back – but we can't stay here and hope to survive."

Hector nodded. But before he could decide his next move a far away rumble of explosions made him turn. For an instant he feared another North Korean attack from his unprotected flank but the eruptions of violent noise had come from further away. Beyond the high walls of the complex, he could hear the sounds of the battle along the death-choked highway still raging furiously. Two huge black columns of smoke were billowing into the morning sky and there was more smoke rising from further along the road. He sensed the attack into the heart of the industrial estate was bogging down. He turned further and peered back through the breach in the wall, through the sifting skeins of smoke and dust-filled air.

"Where's the Abrams?"

"Long gone," Breevor said.

Hector turned his attention back to the fight in front of him. The narrow alleys between the buildings were choked with North Korean dead and wounded. Some men lay groaning in puddles of spreading blood. In a shattered doorway a man screamed, clutching in horror at his guts. The dead were piled in untidy mounds.

Then the North Koreans attacked again.

They came pouring from between the buildings, scrambling over the tideline of bodies who had fallen before them, firing wildly and screaming shrill oaths of death. They came in a ragged mass, without cohesion, propelled forward by their fanaticism. The survivors from the first wave scrambled from their cover and joined the attack, adding their blood-curdling screams and firepower to the tidal wave of bodies.

"Fire!" Hector shouted. "Don't let them close on us!"

Officers and Sergeants in the midst of the North Korean attack shouted to urge their men forward. The bugle sounded from somewhere beyond the horde. The shouts turned into cheers as the wave of enemy soldiers seemed to loom over the Americans, moments away from overwhelming them.

Hector went cyclic on his M4, hosing the weapon in a scything arc. The range was so close that he could not miss.

The fury of the battle reached a crescendo of shouts and screams and hammering automatic weapons fire.

A North Korean clambered over the body of a fallen comrade and fired his weapon at an American crouched at the corner of a building, hitting the man in the knee. The wounded soldier howled in agony. He tried to rise to his feet to find new cover but his leg collapsed beneath him and a North Korean lunged with a bayonet. Hector fired and hit the enemy soldier in the small of the back. The man arched his spine and reached behind him as if he could pluck the bullet from his flesh, then fell to the ground and didn't move again. Two Americans dashed forward and dragged the wounded man to safety.

Then – just as it seemed inevitable that the 'Culprits' must be overwhelmed and slaughtered – Lieutenant Richard Curry and the men from 2nd Platoon burst through the breached wall and saved the Company.

The Platoon stormed through the ragged hole in the wall, firing on the run and supported by the two M240B/L machine guns. Curry led the attack, surging into the slaughteryard of smoke and bullet-torn air, urging his men forward. The phalanx of automatic fire slammed into the head of the North Korean charge and crushed it in five savage seconds of fury. The two groups of soldiers were close enough to smell the spattered blood and the mingled stench of sweat and fear. Men cursed and screamed as they fell. A North Korean Sergeant took a bullet to the lung and staggered backwards clutching at his wound and vomiting blood. A man at the Sergeant's shoulder was shot in the hand and lost three of his fingers. He dropped his weapon and clutched the bloody stump under his armpit, then was hit by another bullet to the chest that killed him instantly. A sudden panic gripped the North Koreans and the frenzy that had driven them onto the American guns dissolved into chaos. Bullets criss-crossed the blood-drenched courtyard and the smoke hung thick in the air. John Hector sensed the momentum of the battle turn, and he bellowed into the maelstrom.

"Fire! Keep hitting the mothafuckers!"

A Corporal standing a few feet away from Richard Curry was shot in the leg. A medic dashed through the debris. He hooked his hands under the man's armpits and dragged him into cover. "I'm gonna die!" the young American wailed, trying to staunch the pain. His lower leg was awash with blood. "I'm gonna fuckin' die!"

"Shut your mouth!" Sergeant Breevor cuffed the young man across the head. The wounded soldier was one of the new recruits who had joined the Company just twenty-four hours earlier. "Your shouting is pissing me off. It's nothing but a fuckin' scratch."

"I'm bleeding out!" the young rookie moaned. He was stricken with fear, tears of pain rolling down his cheeks.

Breevor pushed the medic working on the wound aside and snarled at the bleeding man. "I said shut your fuckin' mouth. And if you don't, I'll shoot you myself."

The young recruit blinked in shock and fell into an uneasy silence. Breevor turned back to the battle and emptied his magazine into a knot of enemy soldiers that had broken away from the main group. Four North Koreans went down in a tangle of blood and broken bodies. A gunner on one of the SAWs finished the wounded off, then swung his aim back to the milling enemy. The North Koreans were caught in a no-man's land of hesitation. They could not press home their attack; the massed firepower of the Americans was too overwhelming, but nor could they fall back for there was nowhere to retreat other than into the bomb-devastated ruins of the nearby factory buildings. A cluster of enemy soldiers made a final fatal charge and were scythed down by a prolonged merciless fusillade of machine gun fire.

When the smoke cleared and the dust began to settle and the rattle of light arms fire had become a desultory spatter, the North Korean attack lay broken and bloodied to a pulp. Here and there men still writhed in pain. Some survivors had been buried beneath the dead bodies of their fallen comrades. Their cries for mercy, for aid and for water were ignored.

John Hector rose from behind the rubble that had sheltered him and surveyed the slaughtered ruined bodies. The grimace on his face became frozen, baring his teeth and slitting his eyes. He had seen too much death, too much brutal savagery to be touched by the carnage. He wandered through the smoke and all he could see from one end of the complex to the other was dead enemy bodies.

Richard Curry reloaded his weapon with a fresh magazine and came forward warily, stumbling over corpses and splashing through blood. Hector looked the young Lieutenant up and down with a tinge of respect. Curry had stormed into the fight when it was at its fiercest and had emerged unscathed.

"That was a fuckin' stud thing to do," Hector nodded his approval. "Hooah!"

"Hooah!" Curry responded. His face was black with caked layers of dust and grime so that only his eyes showed white.

There was no time to reflect on the aftermath of the battle, no time even to count the dead or care for the wounded. They would be left for the medics to tend to. Hector checked that his weapon was loaded with a fresh magazine and then led the 'Culprits' through the maze of factory buildings, his eyes scanning for more enemy troops and an exit that would open onto the highway. The 'Culprits' still had a factory to seize and a fight to win.

Chapter 8:

Hector led the remnants of the company towards a set of high wire gates through which he could see the highway and their target building in the distance. The factory lay a mile further along the road, and on the opposite side of the blacktop. The building was wreathed in smoke and obscured by flames. Hector sent three men forward to open the gates while the rest of the troops took up overwatch.

The sky was criss-crossed with smoke trails, the air trembling with the incessant sounds of explosions and gunfire. The noise rose to a furious snarl and then ebbed, only to rise again. Gayle Nordenman came scurrying across the concrete tarmac, running doubled over.

"Are we pushing on towards our objective?"

"Yes," Hector said without hesitation.

The gates were flung open and the Company moved forward. On the sidewalk Hector glanced left, back towards the outskirts of the industrial area to get a fix on the Brads and to gauge the progress of their advance. What he saw struck him like a punch to the guts. The Company of mechanized infantry had been slaughtered to a man. There were dozens of dead bodies littered across the highway. They lay in dark crumpled heaps around the burning ruins of their vehicles. Not a single Bradley had made it beyond the first five hundred yards of highway. Hector saw half-a-dozen twisted metal carcasses burning fiercely, debris and flung metal strewn across the road. One vehicle had been blown wide open and burned down to its chassis. Two other Brads lay overturned. One had careened off the road and ploughed into the wall of a building. The vehicle was still ablaze, surrounded by the scattered remains of the men it had contained.

"Christ!" Gayle Nordenman gasped. "They've been massacred."

Hector guessed the Abrams tanks had fared better. They were punching through the enemy's perimeter but doing so unsupported by infantry. Hector could hear their huge main guns firing and the chatter of coax machine guns but he could not pinpoint their location. He figured they were somewhere further west of the highway, caught in a maze of narrow alleys and concrete residential blocks. Unless some of the mechanized infantry had escaped the ambush they had driven into, the Abrams were unlikely to reach 'Culprit' Company anytime soon. No tanker liked fighting in an urban environment, especially without a screen of infantry to clear the route of enemy RPG teams.

Hector hesitated. A few minutes earlier he had been resolved to push on to seize their target factory. Now he was filled with sudden uncertainty. He searched for his RTO. "Get Battalion on the line. Tell them what's going on. Tell them our location and that we're unsupported."

They couldn't remain in the open while they waited for orders. Hector led the Company across the four lanes of open highway towards the shadowed wall of a long one-story factory on the opposite side of the road. It was a brick building with a row of small windows along the facing wall. As soon as the Company revealed themselves, exposed and vulnerable in the middle of the road, enemy troops defending the factory opened fire. The 'Culprits' scattered, scampering for small cover behind flung debris and crumbling walls. A flail of light machine gun fire zipped and snatched at the air. Hector threw himself down in the middle of the highway and returned fire, blazing way with his M4 at a window to suppress the enemy.

A man crouched behind a crumbled chunk of masonry rose and fired at the factory windows, then was thrown to the ground by an enemy bullet that struck him high in the chest. He went down hard in a spatter of blood, writhing on the blacktop and screaming. More bullets flailed through the air, thudding into the wounded man's body until he suddenly went very still. Hector's first thought was that the man was dead. He was lying in a thick spreading pool of blood. Then he saw one of the man's legs twitch in spasm. Hector sprang to his feet and darted to the man's side, ignoring the fury of enemy fire that hunted him. He rolled the man over and the soldier sobbed. His face was wrenched into a grimace of agony. His eyes were screwed shut and there was blood in his mouth and bubbling down his chin. "Carter!" Hector recognized the man from 1st Platoon. "Hold on, man. Just fuckin' stay with me for a few more minutes."

Hector slung his M4 over his shoulder and seized the wounded man by the collar, heaving him towards the bullet-riddled shelter of a burned-out car. The soldier screamed in pain and his body began to convulse. Richard Curry dashed out from behind a crumbling section of brick wall and helped Hector haul the man into shelter. The soldier moaned and a gush of blood erupted from between his lips, spattering Curry. "Oh, Jesus!" the wounded man croaked and took a shallow shuddering breath. "Oh, sweet Jesus…"

A medic appeared, favouring one arm. He had been shot in the left hand. Despite his own injury he dropped to the ground beside the wounded soldier and began to strip off his body armor. The wounded soldier heaved and then lay unmoving. The medic looked up at Hector with vacant eyes.

"He's dead."

Hector unslung his M4 and turned hateful eyes on the factory on the far side of the road. He seized a fistful of Curry's tunic and pulled the Lieutenant towards him. "Find ten men from your Platoon. Get them together and rush the building. The rest of the Company will cover you."

Curry nodded, but Hector wasn't finished. "Go in hard and fast and once you breach the doorway, kill every fucker inside. Understand?"

Curry went jinking away, weaving a ragged path in and out of cover, gathering men while enemy bullets tore chunks from the asphalt at his heels and ricocheted off twisted steel debris.

When Curry had enough men around him, he peered across the smoke-drenched highway at the factory and saw a set of double steel doors, padlocked and chained. The notion of charging across the open road into the waiting jaws of enemy fire was utterly terrifying. Curry felt his flesh crawl with the horror of what he had been ordered to do. Yet he steeled himself and put grim resolve into his voice as he shouted his instructions above the snarl of enemy fire that flailed around him.

A Javelin operator launched a Javelin missile at the double doors and they exploded open in a great gout of flames and smoke. Chunks of steel were flung through the air and the brick wall either side of the doorway blew in, filling the street with choking dust. The ground beneath Curry's feet trembled as debris went cartwheeling into the air.

"Now!" he shouted and sprang to his feet, his legs stiff and cramping, his heart thumping wildly in his chest. The men around him scrambled forward, running at his side into the wall of smoke and dust. Somewhere nearby there was an explosion and the shattering force of the eruption buffeted Curry off his feet. He got to his knees, pushed himself upright, and kept running.

Time seemed to slow so that everything registered with stark clarity. He saw the shattered doorway thirty feet ahead of him, the grey-black smoke swirling in the entrance, backlit by spot fires. He felt the debris scattered across the road crunching under his boots. Dirt, shards of shattered concrete, and chunks of twisted metal littered his way forward. He saw, too, the row of windows, lit with the muzzle flashes of the enemy guns and the slivers of broken glass on the sidewalk. In his ears was the pounding thump of his heart, the sizzle of blood and adrenaline fizzing in his veins and the distant, muted rumble of explosions and pounding feet behind him. He looked up and saw a face in one of the windows; a dark smudged silhouette of one of the enemy troops trying to kill him and he aimed and fired his M4 while still on the run, seeing his bullets fly frustratingly wide of their mark.

Then suddenly he was at the doorway, still alive and trembling like a man in the grips of a fever. There were a handful of others with him. He saw the fear and terror on their blackened faces. The whole world seemed to be just a few smoke-thickened yards of battlefield where bullets criss-crossed and explosions erupted and flames and gunfire and screams overwhelmed his senses.

Curry went through the darkened smoke-filled breach with his M4 at his shoulder, his senses heightened by fear and exhilaration. Two men filed in close behind him, one peeling left and the other right. A roar of gunfire filled the gloom. Muzzle flashes lit the musty darkness. Curry saw three dark shapes silhouetted by the pale light through the windows. The enemy were firing out across the street. Curry sprayed the factory interior with a long withering burst from his M4 until the weapon clicked on an empty chamber. Through the smoke he heard the shrill screams as his bullets hit targets. He snatched for a grenade and lobbed it into the gloom.

"Frag out!"

Two more soldiers pushed past him into the darkened interior, their guns blazing and the hammer of gunfire deafening in the confined space.

Then suddenly the firing stopped and the thunderous sounds of the firefight faded. Curry stumbled across the debris around the breach, clambering over broken masonry and twisted steel beams. Smoke hung like a veil in the air, and the stench of oil and sweat and stale food and blood washed over him.

His ears were ringing, his eyes streaming tears from the smoke. He reloaded his weapon and closed on the enemy bodies that lay beneath the windows. The walls were riddled with holes, the ground littered with hundreds of discarded shell casings. He went to the closest enemy soldier and nudged the dead body with the toe of his boot. The figure on the ground was crumpled into an untidy heap, the uniform soaked in fresh blood. Curry rolled the corpse over with his foot and stared in aghast horror at the young face. The enemy soldier was just a child; maybe twelve or thirteen years old. He had taken three of Richard Curry's bullets in the torso. The young boy's lifeless eyes started up at the ceiling.

Richard Curry felt a sickening surge of grief overwhelm him as the realisation that he had killed children assailed him. He turned away, suddenly overcome with remorse and guilt.

His arms dropped to his side and his expression turned blank with numbed horror.

John Hector came through the wall breach leading the remains of the Company. The men piled inside and went hunting into the darkened corners, looking for more enemy troops. Hector saw Curry's anguished face, the slump of his shoulders and the torture in his eyes. He scrambled through the debris to the rookie Lieutenant and then saw the face of the North Korean child dead on the floor.

Hector flinched as the grimace of his expression became fixed.

"They were kids…" Richard Curry's voice was desolate. "I killed a handful of children."

Hector turned aggressive. He pressed his snarling face close to Curry's and shook the Lieutenant savagely. "See that gun? That's a real fuckin' gun," Hector hissed. "And see those bullets? They're fuckin' real too. If you didn't kill those fuckers, they were going to kill us. I don't care if they're ten or a hundred. If they're carrying a gun, they're the enemy. This is war, Lieutenant, and you better get your head in the game right fucking now. It's ugly, it's cruel, it's merciless… and anyone who points a gun at me or my men is the enemy and they're going to die. Do. You. Understand?"

Curry nodded his head; his eyes still vacant and glazed.

"Do you understand?" John Hector shouted again more savagely. The bellow and violence of Hector's voice cut through the fog of Curry's despair. He blinked, like he was waking up from a nightmare, only the nightmare was real and dead on the floor at his feet.

"I understand, sir," Curry stiffened. His face was white under the mud and grime and there were tears prickling the corners of his eyes. Hector pushed him towards the far side of the factory. "Get your Platoon organized. You'll be leading the drive towards our objective. And do it fast, Lieutenant. We're moving out in sixty seconds."

Gayle Nordenman watched the young Lieutenant stumble away in the far side of the factory. Part of the building's roof had collapsed under the pounding of relentless Allied artillery fire and now the floor was littered with huge sheets of corrugated iron, and fallen roof girders.

"You're being hard on him John," the XO observed tactfully.

"I've got to," Hector said, his eyes hard. "He killed three kids, Gayle. If I let him dwell on that, he'll never recover. He needs to get straight back into the fight – even if it gets him killed."

"You're a hard man…" Nordenman let that comment hang in the air, not sure how Hector would react.

"It's a hard fucking war," Hector snapped back with more spite than he had intended. He stopped himself and took a moment to draw a deep breath before he continued. "If Curry has the time to think about what he's just done, he'll end up eating a bullet. The only cure for drowning in this kind of horror is to be thrown into even deeper water. He'll either be killed, or emerge on the other side of this shit-fight a better warrior. Only time and more combat are going to tell us."

The RTO came stumbling through the debris, his expression simmering and bitter. "Orders from One-Six Actual," the RTO gave the call sign of Lieutenant Colonel Gallman. "We're to push on to our objective regardless of casualties. The factory has to be taken and held until the attack from the west can hook around and relieve us."

Hector grunted and his eyes turned cold with contempt. "Tell One-Six Actual that we need support. The Brad Company has been slaughtered and we've lost contact with the Abrams. We've also been isolated from Delta and Bravo Company. We're on our own here and we've been hit hard by the enemy."

The RTO bent to his radio and relayed the message while Hector, Nordenman and Breevor stood knotted together by a window on the far side of the building from where they could glimpse their objective further along the highway.

The distant factory looked like a fortress; a huge imposing two-story structure with cement-slab walls and two hangar-type door openings. The western end of the building was on fire and a section of the roof had been caved in by artillery strikes. The majority of the building was shrouded in whirling banks of black smoke, revealing only menacing glimpses.

The RTO returned, his expression unreadable. "One-Six Actual says there is no support available. We're to attack with what we have immediately and seize the factory."

*

The remnants of 'Culprit' Company advanced with Richard Curry's men of 2nd Platoon once again at the point of the wedge. The men were spread out and moved in short dashes from cover to cover, going forward into an eerie tense silence.

Hector felt his rising apprehension. The battlefield had fallen into a lull; the explosions and gunfire seemed distant and muted. He could hear the rasp of his breathing and the thump of his heart. He was soaked and dripping sweat, his eyes red-raw and his stomach knotted tight. He could smell the fear and tension amongst his men as they moved like wraiths through the drifting smoke. The thump of running footsteps, the rustle of their uniforms and equipment all seemed amplified as they crept closer to the looming silhouette of the factory.

When they were within a hundred yards of the factory's high wire perimeter fence, an enemy soldier suddenly appeared in the distance from behind the corner of a small outbuilding. He darted out of cover and sprayed a burst of automatic fire from the hip, then ducked back out of sight. The men in the vanguard of the advance threw themselves behind the nearest cover and returned fire. In an instant the fraught silence had been replaced by the thunder of a roaring firefight. The factory was heavily defended. More enemy soldiers began firing from the rooftop and from behind sandbagged walls until the air was thick with a cross-fire of hot metal.

Sergeant Breevor ran forward and threw himself down beside Richard Curry.

"We can't stay here!" Breevor shouted.

Curry looked about him in desperation. There was a narrow alley away to his right that ran between a maze of low-rise worker apartment blocks. Curry called out to his Sergeant.

"Garcia! Take five men down the alley. See if you can get into a flanking position to support an attack!"

The Sergeant gathered a handful of men around him and went jinking laterally, across the face of the battlefield and disappeared into the shadow-struck alley.

Garcia led his fire team through the low, squat buildings and up two flights of an external steel stairwell onto the flat roof of one of the apartment units. From their position they had vital elevation and overwatch abilities. The men dashed to the edge of the rooftop which was surrounded by a low-rise concrete wall. The soldier hefting the SAW set the machine gun down and squatted himself behind the weapon, with the barrel of the SAW hanging over the low wall. Sergeant Garcia pointed the rest of the men to firing positions and then reached for his PRC-119 radio.

From the lip of the low wall, he had an unobstructed view of the factory complex. Through the smoke he saw the main two-story structure surrounded by a cluster of smaller service buildings and an expanse of carpark that was littered with abandoned trucks, forklifts, wooden pallets and steel containers. On the rooftop of the main building he could see a dozen dark prone shapes firing their weapons. The Company was pinned down on the highway leading past the factory gates, returning fire into the rising smoke and chaos. As he watched a Javelin missile streaked through the air and struck the corner of the main building. A part of the brick and concrete wall collapsed in a billow of grey dust and haze.

"Two-Six, Two-Two. We are in position on a rooftop three hundred yards to your west. Standing by to cover the attack."

Curry acknowledged the radio message and rolled onto his side, careful to keep himself concealed from enemy gunfire. He was lying in a mound of white chalky concrete dust, his mouth full of grit. The fire pouring down on the Platoon from the direction of the main factory building was intensifying.

Curry got eye contact with the men huddled in cover around him and shouted his instructions over the roar of gunfire. Quickly the word was passed around. Then the two Company mortars suddenly joined the fight.

John Hector had judged the strength of the enemy and had ordered the mortars to support the impending Platoon attack. The two 60mm mortars were set up in the ruins of a bomb-ravaged building several hundred yards behind the pinned-down men.

The first mortar rounds were HE and they pirouetted in the sky and tumbled down through the smoke. The first explosions fell harmlessly in the factory carpark, but the second salvo scored hits on a small shed fifty yards to the east of the main factory. The third salvo landed at the eastern end of the main building and began to chew fiery holes in the walls and roof.

Curry watched the strike of each mortar and saw the bloom of fireballs erupt from behind grey smoke. He waited two long minutes and then filled his lungs and shouted.

"2nd Platoon, attack!"

The men scrambled to their feet and went forward in a helter-skelter scramble, laying down fire as they ran, jinking and weaving. The mortars supporting the assault changed to smoke cannisters and began to concentrate their fire along the perimeter fence, blanketing the entire factory complex behind a thick white veil of swirling cover.

From the rooftop the SAW and the handful of men opened fire, so that the Company's heavy weapons and the team on overwatch combined tactically to suppress the enemy's fire while the Platoon dashed forward.

Hector watched the assault grind forward and snatched for his radio, ordering 1st Platoon and 3rd Platoon to push forward into the smoke. One of the men wielding a SAW from 1st

Platoon leaped to his feet and sprayed the wall of the factory building with a long withering burst.

Sergeant Ethan Breevor joined the 2nd Platoon's attack, nonchalantly pumping several rounds from his M203 under-barrel grenade launcher into the factory compound and then moving forward with the arrogant strut of a veteran warrior who had stared down death too many times to be scared any more. He dashed to the high wire gates that encircled the complex and blew them open with two grenades. The 'Culprits' poured through the opening and scampered across the open space of the carpark, some men firing from behind abandoned forklifts and the chassis of small trucks at the factory rooftop.

The North Koreans defending the factory fired back, shooting blindly through the thick bank of white smoke, judging the advance of the Americans by the proximity of gunfire and explosions. Several men had died beneath the thundering salvos of mortar fire but those who remained were fanatical in their determination to fight to the bitter death. One North Korean leaped into an open doorway and fired at fliting dark shadows that emerged from the smoke. The Americans fired back, targeting the North Korean gunman's muzzle flash and knocking him down under a whip and flail of counterfire. The North Korean staggered back into the shadows of the factory gushing blood from four wounds. He died in the doorway but was replaced by a comrade who flung two grenades. Four Americans went down as the swirling smoke was suddenly punched apart by an eruption of fire and shrapnel fragments. A Corporal from 1st Platoon had his nose and left cheek flensed from his face, the flesh hanging by shreds of sinew as he was flung to the ground writhing in agony. Another man took shrapnel hits to his thigh and clutched at the pain, teetering for a long moment and then falling sideways into a pile of broken bricks and concrete.

The North Koreans lining the rooftop of the factory building began firing down into the smoke as the Americans emerged, jinking across the parking lot. An old truck with a handful of enemy soldiers crammed into the rear bed of the vehicle appeared from behind the building and swerved wildly across the tarmac. It was an ancient rust-streaked relic from the fifties that had the shape and belching engine of an old Bedford. It came angling across the parking lot with the soldiers in the back firing indiscriminately at the Americans. Hector gaped with incredulous shock and then horror. It was like a scene from an old gangster film. The truck bed had wooden slatted sides and the North Koreans were spraying bullets as the truck careened through the smoke.

Ethan Breevor hosed the runaway truck with a withering burst of fire from his M4 and then one of the SAW operators took aim. He poured a hundred rounds into the rusting relic, killing the man hunched behind the wheel and several of the soldiers on the back of the vehicle, his bullets tearing through the flimsy wooden slats and turning them to kindling. The truck lurched sharply to the left, still travelling at speed, its engine bellowing like a wounded bull, and then flipped over onto its side in a deafening screech of sparks and rending metal. Two Americans dashed forward and fired into the tangle of broken bleeding enemy soldiers while the SAW operator quickly changed barrels on his SAW.

More Americans dashed into the maelstrom of confusion and flying bullets, seeking cover from the overturned truck. Soon a handful of men were sheltering behind the wrecked vehicle's bulk, firing from an enfilading angle at the factory building. John Hector sensed the battle was delicately balanced. The Americans were pouring fire onto the factory but were no longer advancing. He cast a frantic glance around the battlefield looking for inspiration. The air was thick with bullets and choking whorls of smoke. The constant *'crump!'* of grenades exploding and the rattle of small arms fire overwhelmed the sounds of the larger battle taking place beyond the complex so that for a moment Hector felt the 'Culprits' were the only troops still fighting.

Then suddenly a new emerging sound began to overlay the clamor of combat. It came from the south in undulating waves, fading and then growing louder on the air. Hector searched the smoke-stained sky and saw two small black dots in the distance, far away but closing quickly. The helicopters were flying an oblique path across the battlefield. For a moment they disappeared behind a black column of smoke, then re-emerged about a click to the west.

Hector recognized the helos as Apache AH-64s. They swooped low over the skyline then banked further to the west, gradually sliding into the distance. Hector bellowed for his RTO.

"Get Battalion on the line. Tell them we're at our objective but are facing strong enemy resistance. Tell them we need air support asap."

The RTO bent over his equipment and raised Battalion HQ. Hector only half-listened to the broken shouted exchange of messages. The North Koreans were still firing blindly into the smoke but Hector knew that within sixty seconds that shroud of grey drifting cover would dissipate completely, leaving his men in the open and utterly exposed.

The RTO signed off and shook his head. "No go!" he had to press his mouth close to Hector's ear to be heard. "There's no available air support. Everything in the sky is being sent to the west where the attack is stalling."

"Fuck!" Hector snarled. He watched the two Apaches fly through a bank of smoke and disappear.

A man firing from behind a forklift just twenty feet to Hector's right suddenly clutched at his face and howled in pain. A rattle of enemy bullets clanged off the forklift's steel frame in a shower of sparks and metal shards. The enemy were peppering the parking lot, targeting the American muzzle flashes through the smoke. The wounded man dropped his M4 and crouched down into cover and clamped a hand over his face. A bullet had creased his cheek, and he was bleeding profusely. Hector called for a medic and after five seconds without a response he turned in a rage. "Medic for fuck's sake!"

A man dashed forward, his uniform sheeted in spattered blood. He knelt beside the wounded soldier and dressed the wound quickly, then took him by the arm and together they ran in a lumbering crouch towards the CCP (Casualty Collection Point) which had been set up outside the factory gates in a narrow alley. As the medic ran past Hector, the Captain seized the man's arm.

"How are we looking?"

The medic's eyes were blank and unfocussed as though he had sunk into a traumatic kind of shock. His eyes were set deep into their sockets, and his face was spattered with other people's blood. He blinked, then his eyes slammed into focus. "At least fifteen badly wounded, a handful we won't be able to save unless we evac them immediately…"

The attack had stalled and the Americans were being relentlessly picked off. The North Koreans were pouring so much firepower downrange that inevitably they were getting random hits, whittling away at the Americans and stalling their momentum.

Common sense told Hector that he should use the thinning shroud of smoke to fall back into the maze of narrow alleys where his men had good cover. From there they could pin the North Koreans down and wait for support to be sent. But the notion of retreating was galling to his pride – and in a fight, pride was essential.

Without realizing it, Hector sprang to his feet and burst forward, driven on by irrational impulsiveness, anger, frustration and reckless disregard for danger. It was not heroism; it was the fear of humiliating defeat that compelled him.

Seeing their Captain charge headlong towards the factory, the men around him instinctively followed, running into a hailstorm of hot metal. Hector saw two men cut down as they burst through the smoke. One was struck by heavy machine gun fire. Two bullets caught him in the left shoulder, tearing huge chunks from the flesh and bone and severing the soldier's arm. The man crashed to the ground face first, his body flopping in the rubble like a landed fish until he bled out and died. The second man caught a shrapnel fragment in his shin but somehow stayed on his feet long enough to reach the factory's facing wall. He was whimpering in pain, sucking in deep hissing breaths through clenched teeth. His lower leg and boot were soaked in fresh blood, but he refused to give in to his pain. He reloaded his M4, leaning heavily against the wall, his injured leg stiff beneath him and the agony washing over him in waves.

More men reached the factory wall. They burst through the smoke wild-eyed and screaming to give themselves courage. Hector looked about him desperately. There was a side door into the building further along the wall. He began to edge towards it. From a second story window somewhere above them a North Korean soldier dropped a grenade and it exploded amidst the Americans, killing one man outright and injuring three others. Hector made a desperate dash for the door, then wheeled and slammed the sole of his boot into the obstruction, just above the lock. The door slammed back on its hinges and a flurry of enemy fire filled the dark void. Hector reeled back, flattened himself against the wall and lobbed two grenades in through the opening. The sounds of the explosions in the confined interior were appalling, hammering his senses with their force, the searing bright light and the tremendous heat burning furnace-like against his face as he recoiled. The instant after the grenades had exploded into fireballs of flame and smoke, Hector leaped lightly through the door, jinking left and emptying a full magazine into the darkness. Suddenly he felt light and unfettered, freed from the doubts and tactical uncertainty; consumed only by the rush of adrenaline that fizzed in his veins and the demands of immediate action. More men came pouring past his shoulder, knocking him off balance in their terror and fearful haste to clear the way ahead, their guns blazing, the gloomy interior lit up by the flickering tongues of flame from their muzzle flash.

Hector saw the silhouette of an enemy soldier rise from behind a barricade of stacked furniture and he swung his M4 towards the target, frantically reloading and bringing his weapon to bear at the same time. He was a split-second too late. The North Korean fired, spraying the doorway with a scattered fusillade of bullets, hitting the man next to Hector in the chest and knocking him down. Then Hector fired into the unholy chaos of noise and confusion, hitting the enemy soldier flush in the mouth, punching a huge red hole in his face and snapping his head back so savagely that he was thrown to the ground like he had been struck by a giant fist.

Hector danced aside to allow more men to pour through the broken doorway. The building was filled with smoke and shouting. Two more North Koreans came running down a steel staircase from the second floor, spraying automatic fire from their weapons. One of the men stumbled on one of the steps and his weapon discharged into the ceiling. Two Americans pushing forward into the gloom swung their weapons and fired instinctively, killing both enemy soldiers.

"Move it! Move it!" Hector waved his arm, urging more men to spread out and secure the ground floor. He heard a brief exchange of gunfire and the sound of shattering glass, then sudden eerie silence.

"Top floor!"

More troops came surging across the parking lot now that the fire from the North Korean defenders had slackened. They appeared through the smoke in ones and twos, some bleeding and clutching at wounds. Richard Curry led a handful of 2nd Platoon survivors through the door and then thirty seconds later Ethan Breevor and Gayle Nordenman arrived with the rest of the Company following them.

"Top floor!" Hector shouted again. He leaped over the body of a fallen soldier, his boots squelching in the dead infantryman's blood. Ahead of him a knot of Americans were swarming up the staircase, weapons raised, bodies tense and alert for the anticipated hail of enemy fire that would greet them. One of the soldiers flung a grenade ahead of them and in the aftermath of the booming explosion that shook dust and debris from the ceiling, the men burst forward, hammering the air with long bursts of suppressing fire.

Hector dashed through the chaos to join the surge up the staircase, trailing more men behind him. He could hear the sporadic bursts of a firefight taking place somewhere overhead. He swarmed up the steel staircase and saw a dark figure rise suddenly from behind a bank of filing cabinets. Hector fired without thinking, his actions completely reflexive. The enemy soldier ducked back into cover and Hector closed the distance, his face set into a merciless grimace, his jaw clenched and his finger on the trigger. When the North Korean rose again, Hector fired, his bullets tearing the enemy soldier apart, clawing his body to pieces. He dropped out of sight in a gush of spattered blood.

The second story was lit by watery light filtering through the shattered windows. The floor was carpeted and littered with shards of glass. It comprised a maze of open-plan cubicles complete with desks and chairs and typical office furniture. The Americans went methodically down the long central passageway in overwhelming numbers. One enemy soldier cried something unintelligible and then appeared with his hands in the air, trembling and cowered with fear. The American leading the advance shot the man in the chest, then stepped over his dead body and dropped to his knees. There were more enemy troops at the far end of the passage. They were barricaded behind a wall of overturned furniture. The Americans lobbed grenades and charged forward even as the reverberations from each explosion hammered against their ears. They leaped the furniture and hosed the tangle of bodies with rattles of automatic weapons fire.

Hector turned a slow cautious circle, his senses alert. His instincts told him there were no more enemy troops. He cocked his ears and listened hard into the eerie silence, peering through the drifting smoke for flickers of threatening movement. The stench of acrid smoke and fresh blood and sweat assailed his senses. At last he lowered his weapon and the tension went from him to be replaced by a great weary exhaustion; a dreadful weight that turned his limbs to cement and fuddled his brain like a man deprived of sleep. He took a deep breath and a staggering step, the realization that the factory had been captured dawning on him slowly through the daze. His eyes found Sergeant Breevor, and when he spoke, his words sounded drunken and slurred.

"Secure the perimeter," he muttered the order. "And get me a butcher's bill and the RTO. We need to contact HQ and send them a SITREP."

Chapter 9:

A relief column of Stryker ICVs and Bradleys punched through the eastern perimeter of the Kaesong industrial complex just after 1700 hours. The armored column reached the factory that 'Culprit' Company had seized and held throughout the afternoon, bringing with them medical support vehicles, water and ammunition.

The fight for the vast complex was still far from over. To the west, the American advance had been stalled for most of the day and it was only now, as darkness began to approach, that the North Koreans were finally conceding ground and withdrawing north. The sounds of artillery explosions reverberated throughout the long afternoon. The sun turned blood red behind a thick wall of smoke and the wind carried the dust and debris and the stench of death.

'Buff' Loftham brought a handful of captured North Korean prisoners to Captain Hector. The Corporal herded them out through the factory's doors and into the eerie red twilight. They had been discovered in the aftermath of the battle, some of them grievously wounded, all of them still lit with the fanaticism that had compelled them to fight like cornered animals. There were eight enemy soldiers in the ragged column. They looked like dishevelled castaways, their tattered uniforms spattered with blood, gore, dirt and grime. They were unshaven, their features hollow, their eyes sunk deep into their sockets and underlined with dark smudges of fatigue. They shuffled forward with bovine lethargy, their shoulders slumped, shamed by their capture.

They went past Hector slowly, their hands tied. Hector and Nordenman kept their expressions impassive. Seeing the feral state of the enemy troops gave Hector no comfort. It reminded him that warfare was a human struggle. No matter how great the technological advantage one side had, the battle ultimately came down to the will and the resolve of the men who wielded the weapons. The North Koreans were outgunned, and their troops were armed with equipment that might have come off Noah's Ark compared to the hi-tech equipment the Americans could bring to the battlefield. Yet these half-starved urchins with a handful of antiquated weapons had crushed an entire American armored column and fought 'Culprit' Company to the brink of a disastrous defeat.

The prisoners were herded at gunpoint into waiting vehicles for transport to theatre internment facilities and endless hours of interrogation. Once they were gone Hector turned his attention to more immediate problems.

Black Hawk helicopters were circling the sky above the factory, landing one at a time in the carpark to collect the critically wounded. Two Stryker ICVs had taken up hull-down positions on the northern edge of the high wire fence to defend against a possible enemy counter attack. The 'Culprits' went through the factory buildings ransacking them for valuables, food and water. A covered truck at the far end of the parking lot was discovered loaded with unopened crates of Chinese machine guns. Another canvas-covered lorry contained a dozen new Type 69 85mm RPGs which were a Chinese variant of the Russian RPG-7.

"Lieutenant Jakes!" Hector called to the leader of 3rd Platoon.

"Sir?"

"Take your men to the northern perimeter to support the two Strykers. And take the heavy weapons squad with you. If the enemy launch a counter-attack, I want machine guns and the Javelins on the front line to repel the assault." It wasn't much of a force to defend against a concerted enemy assault, but it was the best Hector could manage. At the very least it would buy the rest of the Company time to defend the factory buildings. "And keep the comms line hot. At the first sign of trouble, I want to know about it."

"Well done, Hector," a neatly uniformed Lieutenant from Battalion HQ climbed down from a Humvee. The vehicle had followed the Bradleys through the carnage of bodies and burned-out vehicles strewn along the highway. "Lieutenant Colonel Gallman sends his congratulations."

"Well, that's just what we need," Hector glared at the junior officer with barely-contained contempt. "Fuck the reinforcements I requested, and to hell with the air support I was pleading for. The Colonel's congratulations more than makes up for all the unnecessary dead and wounded men that are going home in body bags or permanently disfigured because he couldn't muster a couple of choppers or a few Abrams when the shit was flying and men were bleeding."

The junior officer flinched like he had been slapped in the face. Hector went on, relentless in his cruel bitterness. "Please pass on my thanks to the Colonel. Tell him from me that I said 'fuck you. Fuck you very much'."

Hector turned on his heel and strode away, his fists clenched and a lump of fury still knotted in his throat. He found Gayle Nordenman on the ground floor of the main factory building supervising the evacuation of three men who had been badly wounded in the firefight. The XO was in the midst of a scrum of frantic medics who were working over the prone body of a man on a stretcher. Hector stared down at the wounded man. His uniform had been ripped open leaving his chest bare. There were wads of blood-stained gauze stuffed into two bullet wounds. The man's flesh was pale and waxen. A medic wearing white rubber surgical gloves was feeding a tube down the wounded man's throat.

Hector recognized the bleeding man and he was overcome with a wave of melancholy grief. He gently pulled Nordenman aside. "Is he going to make it?"

The XO shrugged. "It's doubtful."

"The others?"

"Sullivan and Mayne. They'll be okay, but they're out of the fight."

The two men walked side by side back into the darkening twilight. Hector cast an anxious glance to the west and then the north. The skyline was lit by the flames from more than a dozen fires, and every few seconds there was another explosion followed by a flash of lurid orange light and then a dark smudge of black smoke, adding to the thick blanket of haze that had blotted out the sun and turned the last moments of daylight eerie. The Allied artillery was still in a fury, pounding enemy positions. The North Koreans, too, had begun to shell the industrial complex, bombarding those sectors that had been overrun by the Americans. Hector knew instinctively that at any moment the enemy's artillery would target the factory with its thundering vengeful fury – and there was nothing he could do about it.

"We need to start digging in," he told Nordenman. "Christ knows how long we're going to be here, but it won't be long before the 'crazies' either counter attack or hit us with artillery. Gather all the men that can be spared and get them digging foxholes and filling sandbags around the perimeter."

"Sir!" Sergeant Breevor, who had ghosted silently from the factory's interior, pointed overhead.

Another Black Hawk hung in the sky. It had not come from the south, but instead had arrived from out of the west, appearing suddenly through the banks of black smoke, flying low and fast.

The helicopter was not identified with the red cross of a medivac chopper. It was painted black and unmarked. The pilot set the Black Hawk into a low hover over the factory parking lot and then dropped down out of the sky and landed in a windstorm of blown dust and debris.

As the huge thumping rotors began to spool down, two uniformed men leaped from the cargo bay opening.

The man in the lead was a barrel-chested soldier with the grizzled haggard features of an old alley cat. He moved with the spritely purposeful step of someone in a hurry. Trailing in the man's shadow was the tall cadaverous figure of Lieutenant Colonel Gallman.

"Hector?" the first man out of the helicopter strode forward, his voice gruff and no-nonsense. He wore no rank insignia on his uniform. "I'm General Barett," he extended a big meaty fist.

Hector shook the General's hand. Gallman gave Hector a thin icy smile of acknowledgement but said nothing. The

Colonel looked decidedly nervous. Artillery rounds were still exploding in the distance and the occasional rattle of light arms fire carried on the breeze.

"I just flew in to thank you and your men for their courage and their sacrifice," the General said in a voice loud enough so that the words carried across the parking lot. "Now, get your boys together and tell them to pack their shit. Your Company is coming off the line for forty-eight hours to rest before we push on to Kaesong. I'll have a replacement unit here and ready to relieve you in one hour."

*

Three hours later 'Culprit' Company emerged from the battle for the Kaesong industrial complex exhausted, haggard and blood-spattered. Barely a third of the Company had escaped the fighting unscathed. The rest were being ferried in trucks to aid stations or in body bags to an awaiting graves registration unit. Hector had never known such depths of despair or fatigue. He sat with his men in the back of the transport trucks, bouncing and swaying with each lurch of the vehicle, dozing fitfully, his eyes red-raw and his head impossibly heavy on his shoulders, nodding and lolling to the truck's motion. His mind was numb and his gaze vacant.

No one spoke.

Hector was sweating. Droplets trickled from his brow and into the unshaven stubble that covered his jaw. Beside him Gene Nordenham passed Hector a cigarette. The flare of the lighter illuminated Hector's haggard hollowed features. The two men smoked in silence until the truck finally pulled off the rutted trail beside a knot of trees and braked to a halt. They were four miles behind the lines; far enough away to be out of immediate danger, but close enough to the fighting to hear the percussive explosions of each artillery round that still pounded the northern edges of the industrial complex.

The men climbed down from the trucks, some swaying on their feet. They looked like the damned; stinking, filthy ghouls nearer dead than alive.

Two US Army food trucks were waiting by the side of the trail and the aromas of hot chow washed over the survivors. Freshly uniformed cooks strode amongst the 'Culprits' handing out bottled water. Other men with buckets of soap and hoses climbed amongst the transport trucks, washing blood from the vehicle beds. A couple of chaplains stood clutching bibles and smiling with sympathetic benevolence as the men drifted past them. Here and there a man stopped and dropped to his haunches, sobbing with sudden grief or with delayed shock.

Somehow the men endured the night, sleeping fitfully while overhead artillery rounds continued to streak through the smoke-stained night.

Pain and thirst woke Hector at sunrise. His mouth was thick, his head thumping. He came alert panting and choking from the memory of a nightmare and the terror of it stayed with him until well after the rest of the Company began to finally stir from their sleep.

The day dawned grey with smoke; the sun muted by thick black banks of haze.

A Battalion staff officer picked his way through the prone men, his head turning until he spotted Richard Curry. The officer crouched by the Lieutenant's head. "Sorry to disturb you Lieutenant," the staffer apologized. "But Lieutenant Colonel Gallman has sent for you. You're to meet him at HQ in fifteen minutes."

*

The Lieutenant Colonel's tent was set beside a dirt track on a gentle rise of wasteland about a mile south of the rest area. The tent was covered by camouflage net and surrounded by bomb-cratered ground. As Richard Curry approached, the sounds of the Army shaking itself awake carried on the stillness; a truck roared to life nearby and the muttered voices of thousands of men carried like the far away sounds of a distant heaving ocean. Parked next to the Colonel's tent was the Battalion's M1087 EVAN (Expandable Van Shelter) which was at the heart of the Battalion's mobile TOC (Tactical Operation Center). The vehicle's rear doors were opened and two steel ladders had been set, each leading up to a deck at the rear of the vehicle.

Lieutenant Colonel Benedict Gallman stood at the top of one of the ladders with a mug of coffee in one hand, peering towards the far smoke-smudged horizon. His chin was thrust out, his jaw clenched and his eyes narrowed as though he were striking the pose of an ancient Caesar about to have his portrait painted.

Gallman saw Curry approaching. He waited until the Lieutenant was within earshot before he spoke. "My tent, Lieutenant. I'll be there in a moment."

Richard Curry ducked his head and stepped through the tent opening. The interior was gloomy. He cast his eyes around the small cramped space and saw the glass-encased helmet resting on the Colonel's desk.

"That helmet belonged to General George S. Patton," Gallman had ghosted silently into the tent. He crossed to the desk and ran his hand over the display case with possessive pride. "It was the helmet he wore at the Battle of the Bulge."

Richard Curry sensed he was supposed to be impressed, or at least fascinated. He couldn't muster the energy. He said nothing, and after an expectant silence Gallman went on, his tone suddenly piqued.

"You and I haven't had the opportunity to speak privately since you joined the Battalion," Gallman dropped down into his chair with a dramatic sigh, as though the weight of the war's outcome was a burden he alone must bear. "I reviewed your records. You're clearly a bright young officer with a great deal of potential. I'm sorry you had to be drafted into 'Culprit' Company. You deserved a better Captain and a better group of men."

Curry frowned. He felt himself turn defensive. "I think Captain Hector is an outstanding commander, sir. And the men might be rough around the edges but they're ferocious fighters. I'm proud to be a part of the Company's leadership team."

Gallman smiled thinly, like he was listening to an addled child. "Hector is the worst commander in the Battalion and the 'Culprits' are nothing but the dregs of the Army. They're the bad eggs that slipped through the system. They lack discipline, respect for authority and common manners. If they're not being punished for drunken brawling, they're on charges for theft, looting or disobeying orders. And Hector is a bad influence. You would do well to keep your distance from him. He's not regulation Army. He's a maverick."

Richard Curry stiffened. "That has not been my experience, sir," his cheeks flushed with a rush of hot color. "The men have acquitted themselves bravely and at all times have carried out my orders. And Captain Hector has proven himself a very capable commander."

Gallman grunted. His expression cooled, as though he had suddenly lost interest in the Lieutenant. He reached for a piece of paper on the edge of the desk and picked it up between thumb and forefinger as if it were contaminated. "Captain Hector has recommended you for a medal," the Lieutenant Colonel said as he scanned the page with his eyes, reading small snippets of Hector's report. "For your heroism in the face of the enemy during yesterday's battle – specifically for leading a small group of men into the face of enemy fire in order to overwhelm a heavily defended factory."

Curry arched his eyebrows in surprise and then his face flushed with a surge of gratified honor. "I… I don't know what to say, sir…" the rookie Lieutenant stammered.

"Oh, there's nothing to say, Curry," the Lieutenant Colonel dropped the report into a trash bin. "Because the request is being denied," Gallman said and then got to his feet, hitching his sagging trousers up with his elbows. He came around from behind the desk and his voice turned precise and fussy. "I don't believe in medals, and I don't believe in personal glory," Gallman turned and caught a vain glimpse of his own reflection in a mirror on the far side of the tent. "I believe the Battalion comes first, second and third. We're a fighting unit, filled with fighting men. That's the type of command I inspire, and no one man's personal accomplishments should be highlighted in a group filled with tough soldiers. A Battalion's fighting nature reflects the man who commands it. General Patton didn't believe in handing out medals and the General and I are fighting men cut from the same cloth. We go to war for freedom and for our country – not for personal acclaim."

"I understand, sir," Curry muttered into the horrid silence, keeping his expression neutral.

Gallman went on pitilessly. "Gallant leadership from my junior officers is something I expect from the example I personally set. Heroism is not something I choose to reward with medals."

"I'll keep that in mind, sir," Curry said. His gaze turned blank.

Gallman looked like he might say more, but then changed his mind. He gave the Lieutenant a last lingering look and a final word of warning. "You're a young impressionable officer. You need to decide who you look to for inspiration and who you aspire to emulate. Choose wisely, Lieutenant Curry…"

*

Throughout the day the Allied artillery pounded the retreating North Koreans as they withdrew north to the outskirts of Kaesong city. At 1600 hours Hector and Nordenman were summonsed to Regimental headquarters several miles behind the battlefront. When they arrived, the commandeered building was surrounded with a small fleet of Humvees and Oshkosh M-ATVs.

The steel-framed building had once been a tractor plant. There was an assembly line of incomplete tractors and machinery parts running the length of the vast space with a series of steel steps leading to offices on the second floor. Most of the ground floor had been cleared of clutter and the concrete slab had been chalked with a detailed map of Kaesong.

When Hector and his XO stepped through the open roller doors at the eastern end of the plant, they walked into a cluster of uniformed officers who were being shown the chalked map by several Regimental aides.

Inside the vast cavernous space the sounds of subdued conversation were echoed and amplified. When a sudden blast of a whistle cut through the hubbub, all heads turned to the direction of the sound.

Standing on a steel gantry overlooking the ground floor expanse, General Barett leaned on the support railing and peered down into the throng of upturned faces. Hector and Nordenman stood at the back of the group their view of the General obscured by the officers in front of them, but the General's voice carried clearly.

"No doubt each and every one of you have been wondering when the next phase of the assault will begin and what our objectives will be," Barett began in the same voice he used to address parade ground assemblies. "Some of you might be under the impression that the enemy are beaten and the drive into the heart of North Korea will be a cake walk. Let me assure you, that will not be the case."

The General paused for effect, and then his address lost some of its formality. Suddenly he became more animated. "Kaesong city is the linchpin in the enemy's defensive line. We've done well up to this point to repel the enemy's attack on Seoul and we've pushed them back into their homeland. We have them backpedaling. With the fall of the industrial complex, the last significant obstacle between us and the capital is a few miles north of us. If we can capture Kaesong city, the route to Pyongyang will be thrown wide open."

There was a murmur of voices from the audience below him, but Barett let the noise wash over him. He held up his hands and obediently the silence returned.

"We can't give the enemy a moment of respite. We must push on while we have momentum. We can't be delayed by weather or by waiting for reinforcements. Every hour we hesitate is another hour the enemy has to fortify their new positions and another hour that Chinese reinforcements might arrive to support their North Korean comrades," Barett paused again. The decision by Allied Command to continue the attack had not been easily arrived at. Military doctrine said that before the Allies could advance, they should first secure their supply lines and re-equip depleted units with fresh troops and more equipment. But a buildup on such a massive scale could take weeks; weeks of waiting and inactivity that would allow the North Koreans and Chinese to turn Kaesong into a fortress. Barett himself had been one of the many reasoned voices urging Allied Command to continue the attack north immediately, staking his career on a gut instinct that told him to attack now was a better option than waiting.

Now thousands of American lives would be put on the line and brave battle-weary men would be compelled to advance, once again, into imminent danger.

"The attack on the outskirts of Kaesong city will begin at 0700 hours tomorrow," Barett made the announcement. "I'm confident that we have the firepower and the resources to break the enemy's back. Winning at Kaesong will go a long way towards winning this war so we must be ruthless, we must be relentless and we must be committed to victory."

If Barett was anticipating a rousing round of patriotic applause or an outburst of impassioned cheering, he was disappointed. Down on the factory floor, the Captains, Lieutenants, Intelligence officers and artillery commanders remained eerily silent. They had seen too much blood and gore, too much death and destruction to recognize this next phase of the war as anything other than a brutal grind of steel and slaughter.

John Hector glanced around the assembled officers and saw the subdued frowns on their faces. In the midst of the throng, he caught sight of Lieutenant Colonel Gallman. Hector watched the other man's face. Gallman looked pensive and fraught with worry.

"My S2 says the Chinese are already streaming towards Kaesong from the north in huge numbers," Gallman lifted his voice to ask the General his question. Heads in the crowd turned to identify the speaker, putting the focus on Gallman for a brief moment. "Has Regimental Intelligence got an update about the number of Chinese we can expect once the fighting starts, sir?"

Barret swatted the question away with a gruff growl. "No further update," he rumbled. "And it's irrelevant. We fight and we kill every enemy soldier in front of us, regardless of his uniform. Chinese, North Korean… we don't win the war until they're all dead."

Gallman's called-out enquiry prompted several more questions from the assembled officers. Barret answered them all with the same terse responses. At last, the assembly were organized into smaller groups and each one appointed a 'tour guide' aide from Regimental HQ. Each group was directed to the large plan of the city drawn out on the floor, and shown their objectives. The map worked as a massive sand table. Spread out across the gridded expanse were red wooden blocks denoting suspected enemy positions and red taped 'Xs' that identified suspected North Korean anti-tank emplacements. Allied reconnaissance drones and high-flying spy satellites had been operating non-stop for the past forty-eight hours to locate enemy positions. Everything the Allies knew about the enemy's dispositions was marked on the floor.

On the southern outskirts of the city were the blue wooden boxes that identified each American unit taking part in the battle. Blue taped lines marked their routes of attack through the city's perimeter and a series of tennis balls had been used to identify key objectives.

There were a dozen officers in Hector's group, including Lieutenant Colonel Gallman. 9th Battalion would be one of three infantry units advancing into the eastern districts of Kaesong. 'Culprit' Company's objective would be to seize and hold a key roundabout named Namdaemun.

Namdaemun was the south gate of the ancient walled city of Kaesong. The original gate had been built some seven hundred years ago. All that remained of the historic landmark was an arch set into a section of stone wall that was topped by a wooden pavilion. The ruins were surrounded by a two-lane roundabout that was a key arterial road into the heart of the city. The Regimental aide handed Hector two satellite photos of his objective. He studied them carefully while Nordenman scribbled notes.

When the two officers returned to 'Culprit' Company, it was already dark. Hector went through a detailed Warno with his command team with Gayle Nordenman filling in the blanks, reading from his scribbled notes. When the briefing was completed, Hector took a long moment to gather his thoughts before addressing the officers knotted around him with a final salient point.

"I'm not going to piss in your pockets," he said, staring each person in the eye in turn. "We've left a trail of dead behind us from the outskirts of Seoul to this spot right here. They were good soldiers. Tomorrow is going to be bloody and brutal. If you're waiting for a rousing speech about valour, heroism or freedom, you've come to the wrong place. Tomorrow's battle is not about any of those things. We fight because we have to and we fight for our friends and our buddies. We're a brotherhood so we fight for each other, and we do our best to survive. Hooah?"

"Hooah."

Chapter 10:

The dawn came with a flush of daylight in the east that spread slowly across the sky, fingers of pale light touching the treetops and the mountain peaks. The men of 'Culprit Company' crouched in the shadows, waiting for the moment they would be ordered forward. Kaesong city was a blur of soft dark shapes in the distance, shrouded in wreaths of smoke from overnight artillery fire.

John Hector glanced over his shoulder and saw the columns of parked Brads and Strykers that would carry the mechanized infantry to the city's outskirts. 'Culprit' Company would follow the AFVs into the battle, only dashing forward after the initial breakthrough had been made. The Brads sat, squat steel boxes on the side of the road, their engines idling, diesel exhaust hazing the sunrise. The Companies of mechanized infantry that would be carried to the battlefront were sitting and standing in tight knots, smoking cigarettes. They were infected with a nervous agitation that made their movements jerky and their voices unnaturally loud. One of the men laughed and Hector heard it as a brittle sound, laced with anxiety. Another man struck by bowel-churning terror dashed urgently into a nearby clump of trees to relieve himself.

The morning sky seemed to crack apart with the roar of low-flying A-10 Warthogs. A flight of four of the hunched, unlovely silhouettes passed over Hector's head, flying nap-of-the-earth as they darted north.

Most of the bombing work had been done by F-18s in the hours before sunrise. Hector watched the A-10s streak north and then disappear behind the smoke haze. A few seconds later the morning stillness was ripped apart by the echo of the Warthogs autocannons peppering buildings along the city's perimeter. The aircraft were only over the target for a handful of minutes, then gone again, one of the Hogs trailing grey smoke but flying steadily.

The artillery began five minutes later, filling the air with the shrieking scream of rounds tearing the across the sky. Hector rose and scrambled to the top of a small knoll. With binoculars to his eyes, he studied the fall of the shells and saw the cityscape suddenly lit with the vivid orange flashes of dozens of fireballs, followed by rising columns of black smoke. A second after each fresh explosion, the disjointed sound of the eruption followed, delayed by distance so that the flashes and thunderous roars became like an out-of-sync soundtrack.

The artillery worked along the city's outskirts, traversing from east to west, chewing up buildings and flattening entire suburbs of ugly apartment blocks, leaving a wretched trail of destruction in its wake. Other soldiers in the Company came to watch; a half dozen men staring slack-jawed into the distance as the thunder and roar of explosions went on until the sun was well above the horizon and the impact of each fresh round could be clearly seen.

"I hope they kill every last one of the fuckers," Buff Loftham stared dispassionately into the distance with one hand on his hip and the other holding his M4. His tunic was open to the waist, his chest smeared with sweat and grime. None of the soldiers had showered because there was no water to spare. They were unshaven, red-eyed and unkempt. Their clothes were spattered with mud and blood, and many were splotched with cuts, scrapes and livid red infections. They stank; a rancid odor of locker-room-like unwashed funk. Loftham swished his mouth out with water and scraped the back of his hand across his stubbled face. "But if there's anyone left after we bomb the fuck out of 'em, I hope I get the chance to finish the job."

A couple of other men chorused the big Corporal's sentiment, but they were half-hearted. They'd seen too much of war to still be filled with bravado. They had begun the fighting in Seoul as gung-ho warriors. Now they were survivors.

Hector peered beyond the nearby knot of men and swept his eyes across the rest of the Company. They were sitting in small groups by the side of the road with quiet patient acceptance, waiting to do the deadly work that must be done. With a small shock, Hector realized he could barely recognize more than twenty familiar faces. Overnight thirty fresh recruits from Seoul had arrived to bolster the Company's withered ranks. The rookies were freshly uniformed and fresh-faced, unsure of themselves and trying without success to hide their rising terror. Sergeant Breevor was walking amongst the ranks, stopping to share a brief joke and dispensing snatches of tough love the way a good Sergeant should. Breevor carried his M4 in one hand and spare ammo magazines in the other. His face was streaked with mud so that he looked like he was wearing camo paint. Through the mask of grime only his teeth and eyes flashed white. Breevor saw Hector following him with his eyes and he gave his Captain a casual nod, as if to reassure him that when the shit went down, the men would be okay; he'd make sure of it.

Hector inclined his head, then spun around sharply because suddenly the mech infantry boys were mounting up. All along the line the Brad drivers began to rev their engines and a couple of officers appeared, yelling orders and infecting everyone with their urgency.

Hector watched the Brads rumble into action. One by one they pulled onto the blacktop and picked up speed, loaded with their cargo of soldiers. They formed up on the highway and then at exactly 0600 began to dash forward, driving at full-tilt towards the distant pall of grey smoke. A minute behind them followed a convoy of Stryker ICVs. Hector turned away to shield his eyes from the thrown dust and debris kicked up by the vehicles as they whooshed by.

"You reckon the arty has done the job?" Gayle Nordenman came swaggering towards Hector. The XO looked unphased by the prospect of imminent combat.

"No," Hector said.

"Well, they've certainly pounded the shit out of the outskirts," the XO said. "I can't remember the last time we threw so much arty at the enemy before an attack."

"It won't matter," Hector said soberly. "The fireworks won't count for shit. Half the 'crazies' will be burrowed down deep and waiting for the attack. It won't matter if everything has been flattened, they'll still be there in the rubble. We know that, Gayle. No point thinking it will be any different this time."

Nordenman shrugged. "Well, we will know for sure in about sixty seconds," he glanced at his watch and then at the columns of Brads and Strykers dashing into the distance trailing a skirt of swirling brown dust. "If there are any 'crazies' left in that mess, they're going to open fire on those APCs any minute now…"

Both men turned and watched. Hector put the binoculars to his eyes and focussed on the lead Company of Bradleys. They were in echelon formation, the lead vehicle hurtling down the center of the blacktop. Hector felt himself tense. Silently he urged the Brads on, praying they might reach the city's outskirts undamaged. He swung the binoculars ahead to estimate the distance and figured there was less than a mile of flat open ground left to cover – and still the Brads were storming forward, billowing black exhaust in a suicidal charge towards glory.

"They're gonna make it," Nordenman urged the APCs on like he was cheering a racehorse to the winning post. "Less than half a mile –"

Suddenly the distant outskirts of Kaesong lit up with flaring jets of muzzle flash and swirling pythons of grey smoke. The lead Bradley was struck flush on the front of the hull and disintegrated into a million fragments. The fireball of the explosion swept over the following vehicles and engulfed them in black roiling banks of smoke. Then another Bradley took a hit from an RPG7 and stopped dead in the dirt, the front of the vehicle crumpled and the nose down, buried in the ground. Another Brad swerved to avoid the carnage on the highway and was hit broadside by an RPG rocket. The projectile struck the vehicle's tracks and obliterated two of the running wheels on the left side. The vehicle slewed to a halt, wreathed in smoke and the men it was carrying stumbled out into the chaos.

The Brads started firing blindly into the distance, adding to the confusion. A Black Hawk helicopter that had been circling in the sky well behind the Allied lines suddenly dashed forward. An enemy SAM missile launched at the helicopter from somewhere deeper inside the city. The Black Hawk pilot saw the incoming enemy missile and put his chopper on the deck, swirling and jinking in a desperate attempt to lose the missile. As the chopper swooped over the highway the missile veered across its path and clipped the tail rotor. The Black Hawk went spinning crazily across the sky, disappeared behind a veil of smoke, and then hit the ground in a fiery explosion.

Two more Bradleys took hits from North Korean RPGs and two more AFVs were blown to pieces by what Hector guessed was an old enemy T-62, or maybe a T-72, although he could not pinpoint the enemy vehicle's firing position in the swirling smoke-drenched madness. The boom of the heavy gun shook the air and a split-second later one of the Stryker's was hit. The vehicle took the round broadside as it swerved off the road. The hammer-blow impact of the HE round tore the front end off the vehicle and the subsequent explosion and hail of shrapnel killed every man aboard.

"Christ!" Hector stared in despair at the carnage. He put the binoculars down and looked on impotently. He could see mechanized infantry spilling from their vehicles and milling about in the turmoil of noise and smoke and fire. They were scrambling to take up firing positions but there was no cover. The gallant armored advance had been smashed to pieces by the enemy and now the attack was stalled and in danger of annihilation.

The RTO snatched at Hector's arm. The man's expression was appalled. "We've been ordered forward immediately, sir," the man said. "The General's orders. We go forward, link up with the mech boys, and push on to the city's outskirts."

"God help us," Gayle Nordenman breathed.

*

Someone in command had the sense to order a barrage of smoke to conceal the infantry as they advanced and to shield the survivors of the armored column that was being smashed to pieces by enemy resistance. Hector led 'Culprit' Company forward. It was a mile across open grassy ground to reach the remains of the armored column and then another half mile of hell to the bomb-ruined outskirts of Kaesong.

The Company advanced in loose formation, spread on either side of the highway. Shrapnel fragments whizzed and hissed through the air and the smoke hung low to the ground like a thick choking fog.

"Spread out, for fuck's sake!" Hector kept his head turning from side to side as he went forward at a running crouch. Despite the maelstrom of noise, he could hear his ragged breath loud in his ears and feel the tripping thump of his heart. A wall of heat and smoke washed over them and then they were in the eye of the storm, surrounded by almost twenty blackened Strykers and Bradleys, with dead and wounded men scattered across the blacktop. Hector saw a soldier lying face-down in a stain of dark blood. His legs were missing and the left side of his body had been blackened by flames. The sickly-sweet cloying stench of burning flesh lodged in the back of Hector's throat and made him retch. Some men were screaming in pain, clutching at gruesome disfiguring wounds. Others sat stunned and uncomprehending in the dirt, concussed and disorientated. One soldier was kneeling behind the mangled wreck of a Stryker blazing away with his M4 at the far skyline, screaming his fury like a berserker.

Hector peered into the smoking chaos and quailed. No one seemed to be in command, and in the absence of leadership the survivors of the mechanised column had broken into isolated pockets, each one trying to find cover and a target.

A man with a face masked by blood staggered dazedly past Hector. The man's eyes were filled with horror and his mouth hung open. He had been struck in the forehead by a piece of jagged shrapnel. The chunk of steel was still buried in his flesh. He fell into the arms of one of Hector's men and his legs collapsed beneath him.

"Medic!"

Ethan Breevor's huge bellowing voice cut across the frenzy of explosions, calm, confident and impatient. "Keep moving forward you bastards!" Hector heard the Sergeant though he could not see the man through the swirling smoke. "Hurry up, god-damnit! Jenkins, you ugly fucker. Get your ass out from behind that fucking Stryker and push forward. Go! Go! Go!" Somehow Breevor's tone managed to convey his irritation and impatience as though the 'Culprits' had disappointed him by seeking cover instead of pushing forward to the city's outskirts. "Move it!"

A Corporal tripped over the entrails of a dead man and fell into the bloody muck of the corpse's eviscerated remains. A rookie soldier who had just joined the Company the night before lost his left arm when an enemy RPG exploded against the hull of an already-burning Bradley. Hector looked around him and saw nothing but chaos and carnage. The attack had gone to hell in a handbasket and now the fire from the city's outskirts was intensifying as enemy small arms and light machine guns added their roar to the clamor.

Ahead of Hector was just a grey drifting wall of smoke, obscuring the city and disorientating him. He got down low behind the ruins of a Bradley and beckoned for an RTO with an urgent wave of his arm.

The woman dashed to Hector's side. The left side of her face was spattered with someone else's blood. Hector seized her by the arm; his grip like a vice. "Get on to Battalion HQ and tell them we need more smoke. Tell them I estimate fifty percent mech infantry casualties. Tell them I'm not going forward until the smoke is thick as soup. And tell them we need those Hogs back in the air for fuck's sake."

The ramp of the immobilized Bradley was down in the dirt. The radio operator ducked inside the ruined shell of the vehicle for cover and hunched over her gear. There was a dead man lying slumped on the steel floor of the vehicle, the back of his head missing and his body sticky with blood. There was more blood dashed against the steel interior walls. It looked like the scene of a slashing murder.

From where he sheltered, Hector could hear the woman shouting across the comms, trying to get through to Battalion. He blocked the sound of her voice out and focussed on the firefight. The remnants of the mechanized infantry were lying prone in the dirt behind small furrows of ground or tufts of long grass. The 'Culprits' were scattered amongst the mechanized infantry and everyone was blazing away blindly, firing through the thinning smoke. It was panic fire, and it pissed Hector off. He knew all the men were doing was wasting ammunition but there was no way he could make himself heard above the whip and roar of the fighting.

Then a new sound joined the fight; the muted *'crump!'* of smoke shells landing a few hundred yards ahead. The smoke rounds sounded like far-away fireworks. They landed in a ragged line and bloomed grey-white. Hector swung his gaze skyward, searching the horizon for approaching dark specks that would signal the return of the Hogs, but saw nothing.

More smoke rounds landed, thickening the white haze. The breeze was blowing from east to west, carrying the thick swirling veil across the battlefront. Hector called for Breevor and Nordenman.

The XO and the Sergeant dropped into cover behind the Brad and Hector barked his orders. "We're going forward," he said. "Keep everyone off the fucking road. We're hooking to the west, following the smoke, and moving diagonally towards the outskirts. Tell everyone to hold their fucking fire."

Breevor nodded.

Nordenman looked over his shoulder. They were surrounded by a scatter of dead bodies and the casualty count was rising every moment they delayed. "What about the mech boys?"

"Tell them to go forward with us. Tell them the order is from the General personally," Hector told the lie and Nordenman nodded. The last thing Hector needed in the middle of a firefight was a pissing competition with another officer. He glanced at his watch. "We go in sixty seconds. Breevor, get the HMGs and the mortars set up behind some of these wrecked vehicles. If there are any Strykers or Brads still in service, we need their heavy weapons cover. Just tell 'em to fire until they run out of ammunition, understand?"

Sergeant Breevor nodded. Another dozen smoke rounds landed in the distance and then suddenly there was a lull in the fighting. The three men got to their feet. Gayle Nordenman suddenly folded slowly forward, gasping for breath. The M4 dropped from his hands, and he clutched at his guts. He sagged to his knees, his eyes bewildered and uncomprehending. Blood oozed from between his splayed fingers. He caught sight of Hector, his eyes enormous and his face drained of color. "Sorry, John…" he croaked an apology for getting wounded.

"Medic!" Hector snarled. He dragged Nordenman behind the Bradley's mangled bulk and ripped off his helmet. Nordenman's face wrenched into a spasm of agony and he began to sob and gasp. He groped for Hector's hand and squeezed it tight.

"Medic!"

Nordenman's body heaved in a series of short explosive breaths and then his eyes slammed back into focus and he saw Hector's face kneeling over him. "Fuck… this wasn't supposed to happen…" were his last words. His body went limp, his eyes turned empty, the expression on his face fixed into an eternal grimace of agony. Hector blinked with the small shock of his XO's death and then spun away, the man's final words echoing in his mind.

"This wasn't supposed to happen…"

"Get up and get moving forward!" Hector raised his voice until he was bellowing across the battlefield. There was no time to grieve. That would come later – after the killing and before the nightmares. Breevor and a handful of other Company veterans echoed Hector's call and the 'Culprits' came to their feet and began to advance, crabbing sideways to follow the drifting smoke and more falling rounds added to the haze.

The noise faded. The Americans stopped shooting and concentrated on forcing themselves to go forward into the face of enemy fire. It was an act of uncommon valor; a heroic charge into withering bursts of machine gun fire that hunted through the smoke and killed indiscriminately. Hector saw one of the mechanized infantrymen stagger and then fall. But behind him there were others, pushing forward, compelled by their training and inspired by the example of his stubborn resolve.

"Keep moving! Keep going!"

Every step brought them closer to the outskirts of the city. The enemy fire seemed to intensify and then lull. The smoke around him thinned and Hector caught sight of the first vague grey outline of a building just a couple of hundred yards ahead. All around him men were still falling, still spinning away in agony or sinking slowly to the ground with wounds. Suddenly there was a shrill scream of savagery; an exultant sound that carried on the air and seemed to mute the thunder of enemy fire. Hector looked to his right and saw the huge hulking shape of Buff Loftham, a SAW in his arms and his jaw clenched. "Come on you fuckers!" Loftham screamed like a berserker in a frenzy of blood-lust. "Let's tear them to pieces!"

The roar was picked up by others and the noise swelled until the Americans were cheering, screaming, wailing with madness and terror and triumph. They burst through the last wisps of smoke and reached the first buildings, and the firefight reached a furious crescendo as the 'Culprits' and the remnants of the mechanized infantry Companies stormed amongst the rubble, seeking solid cover and savage revenge.

The Americans emerged from the wall of smoke several hundred yards west of the highway, catching the North Koreans defending that stretch of the city's perimeter by surprise. The 'Culprits' scrambled into the bomb-devastated ruins and split into small teams, ferreting out the defenders with small arms fire and grenades as the fight evolved into a brutal close-quarters melee. The mechanized infantry pushed east and managed to finally secure the buildings around the highway, giving the Allies a toehold into the city. Hector led his men north through a maze of narrow crumbling alleys until they had secured a city block.

The North Koreans defending the buildings along the verge of the highway died hard. The 'Culprits' were in no mood for mercy. In a street fight the Americans had more firepower and more advanced weapons. The 'Culprits' left nothing to chance. Each enemy machine gun nest was overwhelmed with mortar fire, grenades and smoke. One by one the enemy pockets of resistance were wiped out as the 'Culprits' began to cut a narrow bloody path towards their objective. A Sergeant from 3rd Platoon stumbled upon four enemy soldiers scampering along a laneway. One of the North Koreans had a heavy machine gun slung over his shoulder. The enemy troops were falling back and searching for a new position to fire from when Sergeant Roswell blundered into their path and reacted instinctively, swinging his M4 onto the knot of North Koreans and shooting from the hip. He emptied an entire magazine into the enemy soldiers, killing all four of them and spattering the nearby walls with their bloody gore.

Ethan Breevor led an attack against a group of enemy soldiers that were barricaded on the ground floor of a bomb-damaged apartment block, first directing mortar fire onto the building and then rushing the doorways behind a handful of grenades. Two 'Culprits' were wounded in the attack before the enemy position was overrun and the defenders slaughtered.

Hector turned and searched the mess of rubble and ruin for a radio operator. "Tell Battalion we have secured the outskirts and the highway into the city," Hector's ears were ringing from the echo of multiple grenade explosions so that his words in his own ears sounded muffled. "Tell them the mech boys are digging in on either side of the highway and awaiting reinforcements. We are driving forward towards the Namdaemun roundabout."

Hector left the RTO and scampered past the crumbled corner of a ruined building. Rubble and debris were piled up along the street's sidewalk. He flung himself down in the tangled ruins and peered forward. Across a wide intersection, he recognized a building he had seen in satellite imagery. It was the next obstacle to be overcome during the Company's advance. Hector whistled loudly. Ethan Breevor and Richard Curry appeared a few moments later. The Sergeant's uniform was splashed and splattered with fresh North Korean blood. Hector pointed. "That's our next objective," he indicated the building to Breevor and Lieutenant Curry. It was a cement-slab apartment block; a six-story tenement of small rooms that typically housed hundreds of residents. Now the building was deserted, the western wall chewed away by an artillery strike and the rest of the structure teetering precariously, as if on the brink of collapse. Breevor grunted.

"Another artillery hit and the whole damn thing will come down," he observed. "Wanna pepper it with the mortars, or tell FIST to call in some Paladin fire? It would save us a hell of a lot of risk-taking."

Hector pressed binoculars to his eyes and carefully scanned the façade of the apartment block. The concrete shell of the building was pock-marked from machinegun fire and shrapnel fragments. On the footpath in front of the building was a high hill of rubble and waste and smashed glass struck through with twisted steel beams. Hector focussed the lenses on the ground floor and then a dark shape, half-concealed by the building's side wall, caught his attention.

"Is that a UAZ with a pennant?" Hector asked, not trusting his eyes and his voice incredulous. He handed the binoculars to Breevor and pointed. "Beside the building, covered in dust."

Breevor scanned the ruined apartment block. He saw what looked like an old WW2 jeep with a canvas cover. From the left front corner of the vehicle's hood rose a thin whip-like aerial and affixed to the top of the aerial was a colored pennant the size of a handkerchief.

"You think that belongs to a high-ranking officer?"

"Maybe," Hector grunted. He took the binoculars back and scanned the ground floor of the apartment again. He could see no obvious signs that the building was occupied, or fortified…

"Curry? Are your boys up for another fight?"

"Yes, sir," Richard Curry replied.

"Okay… then we're going for it," Hector made up his mind.

Breevor said nothing. Richard Curry nodded, his thoughts turning instantly to the imminent danger of another attack.

The three men began formulating a plan but the RTO interrupted them, her voice high-pitched with the importance of her message. "Sir, urgent comms from Battalion HQ. We've been ordered to fall back. The ground attack has failed. The Lieutenant Colonel has issued a general withdrawal order."

Hector recoiled in shock and then unholy fury. "We went through the hell of getting into the city and now they want us to retreat?"

"Yes, sir. Lieutenant Colonel Gallman's orders."

Hector, Curry and Breevor exchanged glances. More good men had died for nothing. Hector shook his head, his tolerance pushed beyond its limits. "No," he said. "No. We're not retreating – not until I find out who, or what, is in that building. Hooah?"

"Damn right," Breevor growled.

The RTO looked mortified. "But sir, we have orders…"

"Fuck the orders," Hector said. "Get back on to the radio and ask HQ to repeat. Tell them we're under fire and only receiving intermittently. Understand?"

"You want me to lie to the Lieutenant Colonel, sir?"

"I want you to stall, Waitley. Just fucking stall him until I find out what's hidden in that god-damned building."

Chapter 11:

Richard Curry assembled the men of 2nd Platoon behind a palisade of crumbled rubble and broken concrete slabs and left them there, crouched in good cover while he crept stealthily to the crest of the rubble heap to recce the apartment building.

Nothing had changed since Hector had given his Platoon the task of storming the building. He could see no movement through the shattered ground floor windows, and except for the rumble of far-off artillery explosions and sporadic light arms fire, the battle for Kaesong city had sunk into an eerie lull. Curry shifted his attention to the route his men would have to take to reach the building. There was just seventy yards between where he lay and the apartment block's front doors. But the path across the four lanes of highway was strewn with debris, the burned out carcass of an enemy truck and a dozen or more dead North Korean soldiers. The blacktop was scorched and spattered with blood, littered with glittering fragments of glass and wreathed in drifting skeins of smoke.

Curry slid back down the mound of rubble and called his men close around him. Hector and Breevor were there, listening with professional attention as the young Lieutenant outlined his plan.

"This isn't going to be a guns-blazing attack. We're going to use the element of surprise. The Company's mortars are going to lob a dozen rounds into the city block on the *far* side of the building. That will get whoever, or whatever is inside the building looking the other way. Once the last mortar round falls, we move out in squads. Do you all understand?"

There were nods and murmurs.

"Mather, your squad will storm through the front doors. King, take your men around the western side of the building where the vehicle is parked and secure the area. Willis, your squad will cover the assault with the two HMGs from the Heavy Weapons squad. If it turns into a shitfight, you open up and give us cover."

Curry checked his wristwatch. He realized absently that it had been thirty-six hours since he had slept. But he was not tired, although every muscle in his body was aching with fatigue, his mind remained sharp and alert.

"We attack on my signal."

He scrambled back up to the crest of the rubble mound, lying flat on his stomach and once again swept his eyes across the façade of the apartment block. A gentle breeze drifted the smoke from a burning building down on him from further along the highway. He could hear the men readying themselves behind where he lay and he felt the first spasm of fear rip through him.

It was the waiting, he realized; those paralyzing moments before the action began and his instinct and training would take over. The Army had taught him how to kill with ruthless efficiency, how to handle million-dollar pieces of equipment… but not how to deal with the anxiety and apprehension when death might be just a few heartbeats away and his fear was so thick in his throat that it might choke him.

A sudden rustle of movement beside him caught him by surprise. John Hector flattened himself in the ruined debris close at Curry's side.

"Are you up for this, Curry?" Hector murmured.

"Yes, sir," the Lieutenant met Hector's speculative gaze with steady eyes, his expression composed.

"Are you scared?"

"Frightened to death, sir," Curry said.

"Good. That means you're ready."

Hector slid down off the rubble mound and Curry followed. Their positions were taken by the squad of men and the Company's two HMGs who would provide overwatch for the attack.

Richard Curry joined Sergeant Mather's squad and began mentally preparing himself for the assault across the highway. Hector sent word to the Company mortars to open fire.

Crouched in the dirt and filth, Richard Curry stared at the faces of the soldiers who would storm the apartment block building. They were all veterans; haggard, exhausted and spattered with grime and guts. Their eyes were red-rimmed but their hands on their weapons were steady.

The first two mortar rounds exploded away in the distance, followed just a few seconds later by two more, each *'crump!'* separated by just a split-second. The sound of each blast was muted by distance and would have been lost in the roar of a firefight if the fighting across the city had not fallen into eerie tense silence.

"Four," Curry counted, and checked his M4 had a fresh magazine and that he had a spare. The man beside him coughed, hacked up a slimy wad of phlegm, and spat into the dirt. One of the other soldiers was passing out sticks of gum.

Two more mortar rounds fell. The sound seemed slightly louder. It might have been a vagary of the breeze, or perhaps the men working the 60mm mortars had made a range adjustment. Again, their first salvo was followed a few seconds later by another bracket of explosions.

"Eight," Curry felt himself tense. He swallowed hard and tightened his grip on his M4. He rose to his feet and moved until he was positioned at the head of the line, ready to lead the attack. The rest of the men assembled around him. One man slapped a mate on the back for luck and someone behind the Lieutenant began to mutter the Lord's Prayer, stumbling through the words because he was in a rush.

The next two mortar rounds exploded and Richard Curry crushed down on a small qualm of terror before it could lodge itself in his chest and debilitate him. The final two mortar rounds exploded and in the aftermath the silence seemed heavy and fraught with menace.

"Go! Go! Go!" Curry rasped the words and burst from behind the rubble mound, running as fast as he could, doubled over and his M4 up at his shoulder, his finger on the trigger as he sighted along the barrel.

He heard pounding footsteps either side of him and the hoarse sawing rasp of ragged breathing. Then suddenly John Hector was beside him, running with the squad, fighting like an infantryman. Curry flinched with shock but said nothing. He pushed on, his boots pounding on the blacktop, the sound of his thumping footfalls so loud in his ears that he cringed. If there was an enemy soldier on guard at the windows of the apartment block, they would be dead in a matter of seconds.

Curry was completely focused on the task, his eyes everywhere at once and alert for the first sign of danger. He felt the peculiar sensation of time seeming to slow until he felt like he was barely moving. He saw glass on the road, and a spatter of dry blood. The tarmac was strewn with empty shell casings, and from the corner of his eye he saw a rat scurry down a drainage grill. Then he was on the far sidewalk and the front entrance of the apartment block loomed ahead of him; the wood splintered and cracked and pock-marked with bullet holes. He turned his head and saw the second squad angling towards the side of the building where the vehicle was concealed and then he put those men out of his mind and focussed all his attention on reaching the doors.

He sidestepped around a pile of bullet-riddled sandbags and the squad tightened up around him, forming into a knot and flattening themselves against the building's wall close to the door. They were crouched, bent double beneath a broken window. Hector was at Curry's left shoulder. Both men were breathing hard, keyed up and pumped full of adrenaline and nervy alertness.

Curry took three deep breaths then spun himself in front of the doors, his right boot raised and all his weight behind the crunching, crashing blow as he kicked savagely and the door exploded violently off its hinges.

The door shattered into a thousand pieces and as Curry pirouetted out of the way, Hector led the rest of the squad through the door, shouting at the top of his voice as he burst into the foyer, the M4 up and pulled into his shoulder, his finger on the trigger and his line of sight straight down the barrel as he swung it in an arc from side to side. He danced lightly to the left and three more men followed him into the open space, each of then shouting, each keyed up, their bodies supercharged with adrenaline and tension. One of the men tossed a smoke grenade into the room and the air filled with swirling haze.

A dark figure scampered across Hector's line of sight, flitting between shadows. Hector tracked the man with the barrel of his M4 and cried out for the figure to freeze. The enemy soldier threw up his arms and brandished an old AK47. Hector was a hundredth of a second too slow. The North Korean soldier fired, hitting Hector in the neck. The impact flung Hector sideways and the M4 flew from his hands as he reeled in the open doorway. Then more bodies were storming past him, shouting, shooting. The interior of the building filled with screams and smoke and in the chaos John Hector fell to the floor, bright red blood gushing from his wound and spilling between his fingers.

He stared up at the ceiling, his eyes misted, his vision blurred. He could feel the wetness of his blood soaking through his uniform. He felt suddenly cold and it became a struggle for him to keep his eyes open. He heard the thunder of pounding footsteps all around him, but the sound was strangely muffled so that it seemed to swirl in his head. He felt his heart thumping, wildly out of control, and his breathing became shallow.

His vision was blotted out by a dark blurred shape and it took all of Hector's strength to keep his eyes open and will them into focus.

"Captain Hector, stay with me sir!" Richard Curry knelt over the Captain and seized his free hand, squeezing it tightly. "Just hold on. The medics are on their way. Just hold on… okay?"

Hector could see the distraught emotion in Curry's young face, hear the desperate plea in his voice, yet Hector felt strangely calm. He had lived by the sword and had prepared himself long ago for the possibility that one day he would die in the same way.

"Was it worth it?" Hector croaked, his voice scarcely more than a whisper.

Curry nodded. "We captured a high-ranking enemy General. He's got more gold braid and ribbons on his uniform than Napoleon," the Lieutenant sounded breathless. "We also captured a handful of his staff and a briefcase full of documents and maps."

Hector nodded. "Anyone else hurt?"

"No, sir."

Hector gave a small gasp and his face contorted with pain and then his eyes screwed tightly shut. The agony washed over him in a crashing wave. Through the fog of his turmoil, he could hear Curry screaming repeatedly for a medic.

Hector squeezed the Lieutenant's hand with the last shreds of his energy and willed his eyes open one last time. "I'm dying," John Hector said. "With Gayle already gone, you have command of the Company, at least until you re-join the rest of the Army…"

"Sir, I –"

"I don't have much time," Hector cut Curry's protest off. "So let me give you a last piece of advice. Look after the men. Get them to safety. That's your priority now. It's the only thing that matters…it's what leadership is really about."

John Hector took a last uncertain breath, and Richard Curry watched his Captain die. The man went with a sigh, as though relieved of an immense burden. His eyes fluttered and then he became eternally still.

Richard Curry stared for a long moment and his eyes prickled with tears. Even though he had known Hector for only a short time, the man's assured confidence had left an indelible impression on the young Lieutenant. He got to his feet at last and the chaos and clamor around him came slowly back into focus until once again he was standing in the aftermath of a battlefield surrounded by screams and shouts, blood and guts.

Ethan Breevor surged through the front door, leading the remainder of 2nd Platoon. He stared down at the prone body of John Hector and saw the blood, then his eyes searched Richard Curry's distraught face as if in disbelief.

"Sergeant," Curry drew himself upright, "Captain Hector is dead. I am commanding the Company until we re-join the rest of the Battalion. I want the rest of the unit brought across the road and this building fortified against an enemy counter attack until we can arrange transport for an exfil."

Breevor flinched, as if it took a few seconds for the orders to register through his stunned disbelief. He nodded his head and disappeared back through the open door. Curry turned and surveyed the rest of the room. The captured North Korean prisoners were kneeling with their hands on their heads, facing the far wall, watched by two armed guards. Curry ordered the uniformed officer separated from the rest of the prisoners. "Make sure nothing happens to him," Curry emphasized the importance of the man. Judging by the four silver stars on his epaulettes, he was at least a General, although Curry had no idea what a man of such high rank was doing at the pointy end of a street battle. What he did know for sure was that the Brigade's S2 would want the man uninjured for interrogation and his briefcase of orders and maps delivered intact and undamaged.

The North Korean officer was dragged to his feet and moved to the southern corner of the ground floor foyer. Curry assigned two more men to guard him and then went around the interior perimeter of the building peering cautiously through windows for a sign of an enemy counter attack. He saw nothing to cause him alarm but his instincts warned him that an enemy assault was imminent. He sent a man to the third floor with a radio and a pair of binoculars and then bellowed for an RTO.

The rest of the Company came filing through the front doors and began dispersing to all corners of the first three floors, taking up firing positions. Curry drew the RTO aside and kept his voice low.

"I want Battalion HQ on the line," he said. "I need to speak to One-Six Actual immediately."

The RTO hunched over her gear and tried repeatedly to get through to Battalion. She looked up at Richard Curry with a pained face of frustration and a helpless shrug. The line was hot with a garble of chatter from other units in the area who were all falling back towards the outskirts of the city, some of them under heavy enemy fire and taking casualties.

"Keep trying!"

It took seven tense minutes before comms were established. Richard Curry picked up the radio and keyed the mike with his thumb.

"One-Six Actual this is Lieutenant Richard Curry," he spoke slowly through the hiss of static. "Culprit Six is KIA. Repeat Culprit Six is KIA. Culprit Five is KIA. I have taken command of 'Culprit' Company. We are in a defensive position and cut off from a direct exfil route by enemy troops. We also have in our possession a high-level enemy asset. Repeat…" Curry relayed the important details of his message again to Gallman a second time to be sure the Lieutenant Colonel had a clear understanding of their situation. "Request an armored convoy to our location," he gave the grid reference and the building's description, "before the enemy have time to mount a concerted counter-attack. Over."

For a long moment there was just static down the line, then Lieutenant Colonel Gallman's voice cut through the interference, his voice cold and clinical, and far from calm.

"Curry? Hector and Nordenman are dead?"

"Yes, sir."

"Your status?"

"Thirty percent casualties, some serious, sir."

"I gave strict orders for the company to fall back almost an hour ago, god-dammit," Curry could hear the rage in the Lieutenant Colonel's voice. "And now you expect to be chauffeured back to safety by an armored convoy? You listen to me, son. You are ordered to exfil your position and withdraw on foot along the highway, back beyond the city's outskirts. Do you understand?"

Richard Curry froze. He could sense the eyes of the men within earshot of the conversation watching him. He remembered John Hector's final words and remembered too the man's unconventional leadership style that seemed contrary to everything Richard Curry had been taught at officer's school. Curry had a decision to make; he could either emulate the defiant attitude of John Hector or toe the line and conform to the military hierarchy's demands for strict discipline and order.

"I understand, sir…," he felt the men's mood turn contemptuous. He saw it in their expressions; the sneer of their derision. "… but, with respect, I don't think you understand our situation. We are in possession of a high-level enemy asset."

"I don't give a fuck!" Gallman's voice exploded across comms. "I ordered Hector to pull the Company out almost sixty minutes ago. Now you're in command so it's your job to make it happen."

"No, sir."

For a moment the line dissolved into an unholy silence. "What did you say, Lieutenant?"

"I said 'no, sir'," Richard Curry sensed the men around him suddenly stir with interest. "I am not prepared to risk the lives of my men, or the life of our high-level military asset by exfiltrating the city on foot. You either send an armored column to evacuate the Company and our prisoners, or I will go directly to the General."

"Curry, you listen to me you little ass-wipe…" Gallman's temper had been frazzled by a day of disaster. None of the Battalion's Companies other than the 'Culprits' had been able to break through the enemy's perimeter. The attack had been an unmitigated disaster and in the washup, Gallman was sure some of the shit would stick to him, tarnishing his reputation and maybe even hindering his prospects for future promotion. Now he had a rookie Lieutenant on the radio disobeying his orders. Gallman lost the last remaining shreds of his control. "If you don't evacuate your position immediately and begin retreating towards the outskirts of the city, I will have you court-martialled!"

"Then nothing else I say or do will matter, Colonel," Curry's voice became fatalistic with resolve. "So let me say this. Fuck you, sir. Send a rescue column to our location or your career will go down the toilet deeper and faster than mine!"

*

When news of the captured North Korean military officer reached Brigade, General Barett became personally involved, ordering a column of a dozen M1126 Strykers into the heart of Kaesong city to affect a rescue attempt. Each of the vehicles was caged in slat armor to protect them against enemy RPG projectiles and flying overwatch would be four Black Hawk helicopters.

The US Army was still traumatized by the events that had taken place in October 1993, when over a hundred elite American soldiers and a convoy of Humvees had tried to seize two key enemy operatives in Somalia. The Battle of Mogadishu later inspired a major Hollywood motion picture and several books. It had not been America's most glorious military moment. Now the General was faced with an eerily similar scenario, and he was determined that history would not repeat itself.

The plan was formulated and the vehicles and helicopters assembled in less than an hour. The Strykers charging into the city had one key advantage over the soldiers who had heroically battered their way through the maze of narrow streets in Mogadishu; the route into Kaesong city was a four lane wide highway and the target building was right beside the road. There would be no labyrinth of alleys to navigate, and no hordes of armed civilians to block their path.

Curry was alerted over the radio that the relief column was inbound. He checked his wristwatch and guessed he had maybe an hour to wait. It was a long time on a battlefield, especially when in possession of a high-value enemy asset. He had to expect the North Koreans would launch a counter-attack attempt to free the officer before he was interrogated and he wondered from where the assault would come. To the north of the building was an urban sprawl of small houses that had been devastated by Allied artillery. Entire city blocks had been turned into an apocalyptic wasteland that the enemy could use under the cover of smoke to creep close to his position undetected. To the west was the highway; a broad grey ribbon of asphalt that would provide a clear killing ground if the North Koreans attempted to storm his position. To the east was a collection of elongated factory and warehouse buildings neatly separated by a network of road and intersections. Part of the district had been pulverised by artillery, and yet through the drifting veils of smoke he could see that many of the buildings were intact.

Curry went storming up the staircase to the third floor and crept cautiously to one of the north-facing windows.

"Anything?"

Sergeant Breevor was ordering men from 1st Platoon into firing positions behind hastily assembled barricades of overturned furniture.

"Nothin'," the gnarly Sergeant sounded disappointed. Curry grunted and peered into the smoke haze, speaking over his shoulder as he surveyed the bomb-ravaged distance.

"HQ has organized a relief column; Strykers and Black Hawks on overwatch. I figure it will be maybe an hour until they reach us."

Breevor knew the high price the rookie Lieutenant would pay for their rescue. Once back at base, he would be court martialled for insubordination, and every other charge Gallman's spiteful, vengeful mind could conjure up.

Curry's career in the Army was effectively over.

"That's good to hear," Breevor said. "The boys will be relieved to get back to base in one piece…"

Curry grunted and turned to make eye contact with Breevor. "I'm not so sure the North Koreans are going to just let us waltz out of here with one of their Generals in custody. I reckon they'll launch an attack to get him back any moment now. We're going to have to fight for the right to hold our ground, I'm afraid…"

*

The convoy of Strykers departed the Allied compound fifteen minutes late and raced towards the outskirts of Kaesong city at high speed. The drivers gunned the engines while each vehicle's commander peered through his periscope searching for danger, rotating the 50cal machine gun that was mounted atop the vehicle and operated by remote control through the onboard Protector M151 Remote Weapons Station.

The blacktop stretched before them, debris and burned-out vehicles littering the side of the road. Here and there lay dead, scorched bodies. As the Strykers blew past, flocks of carrion birds took raucously to flight, disturbed from their gruesome feast.

The Strykers approached the city's outskirts. Wreaths of smoke across the highway thickened and the tension became palpable. They drove through the grey-black pall of haze and into a ghastly alternative universe.

The cityscape looked apocalyptic. Bomb-ruined buildings lined the verge of the highway, their crumbling walls riddled with bullet holes and shrapnel scars, their gutted interiors still smoldering. Here and there spot fires still burned and the air was thick with burning embers and ash. The highway was roadblocked with the blackened shells of destroyed trucks and light infantry vehicles. The commander in the lead Stryker called a warning across the radio to the vehicles in his trail, forcing the convoy to slow down and begin weaving across the tarmac to avoid the litter of debris.

Slowing down made the vehicles more vulnerable.

The North Koreans still defending the main thoroughfare into Kaesong heard the revving engines of the Strykers and prepared themselves to receive the enemy's attack. They were no longer organized into a cohesive fighting force; the American artillery barrage and a day of fierce fighting had eroded their ranks so that now they fought in small, isolated pockets, hidden in the rubble, cut off from their units and isolated without comms. One pocket of four fighters were on the ground floor of a small grocery store on the corner of a road that intersected the highway. When the first Stryker burst through the smoke, one of the North Koreans quickly shouldered an RPG and hastily prepared the weapon for firing.

The first Stryker crawled past the soldier's hiding place and in the distance, he could see a second vehicle emerging from the smoke about a hundred yards to his left. He hesitated, then swivelled at the waist, choosing to fire at the rear of the first Stryker rather than the front hull of the second vehicle.

The operator leaped to his feet and triggered the RPG. The launch tube kicked on his shoulder and the projectile raced across the open space on a wavering plume of grey smoke.

"RPG! RPG!" the commander in the second vehicle had his eyes glued to his thermal sight. He saw the glowing streak of smoke on his monitor and cried the warning instinctively. There was no time for anything other than the moment it took to cry the alert. The projectile struck the lead Stryker and the vehicle was consumed in a fireball of searing flames and billowing smoke.

The cage of slat armor that encircled the vehicle saved the two-man crew from death and the vehicle from complete destruction. The projectile struck the Stryker flush. Inside the ICV the entire nineteen-ton vehicle seemed to rear forward, heaved off its wheels. The sound of the explosion inside the steel hull was like the deafening toll of a thousand bells. Alarms and flashing lights sounded in the chaos that followed as smoke began to fill the interior. The driver pulled the vehicle to the shoulder of the road, its engine still running roughly. His nose was gushing blood. It spattered over his driver's console as he looked about him in dazed confusion.

The vehicle commander radioed, "We've taken enemy RPG damage. Push on to the objective without us."

Over the radio the convoy commander's voice was loud and tense. Captain Robert Grill was in the fourth vehicle in the column, still enveloped in a dense bank of smoke. "Are you operational?"

"Unknown," the damaged vehicle's commander keyed his mike. He could smell diesel.

"Injuries?" Grill asked.

"Nothing significant – a bloody nose and some scrapes."

"Roger that. You're on your own until we exfil. Got it?"

"Roger," the vehicle commander tossed aside the mike and wondered if they'd still be alive.

Captain Grill spoke across the net and ordered the rest of the vehicles to accelerate. To hell with caution. They were in an active combat zone now. A second RPG streaked across the sky and narrowly missed one of the other Strykers.

The commander of the disabled lead vehicle turned the turret-mounted 50cal in the general direction from where the RPG projectile had come from and blazed away. The HMG roared and the entire vehicle shuddered around him. Empty shell casing spewed from the gun and hammered on the hull like a hailstorm.

"Go! Go! Go!" Grill urged his driver. The rest of the column sped past the disabled vehicle, leaving it and its crew by the side of the highway.

The damaged Stryker came under sudden light arms fire as the North Koreans gathered in the shadows to prey on its vulnerability. A grenade bounced and exploded nearby, peppering the steel hull with shrapnel fragments but doing no more damage to the vehicle or the two men inside. A smoke grenade exploded and for a long moment the thermal sights were overwhelmed. The vehicle commander turned the turret and the 50cal roared, firing blindly as the enemy continued to gather in the shadows…

*

On the third floor of the apartment block a rookie Private yelped in fright and then shot a rat as it scurried across the floor. Buff Loftham growled at the man tensely. "You fire your fuckin' weapon at anything other than the enemy again, boy, and I'll wring your fuckin' neck."

The echo of the round seemed to trigger the enemy into attack. A mortar shell exploded against the north wall of the building peppering the ravaged façade with shrapnel but doing no damage to the troops at the windows. Richard Curry sat in the building's doorway, his back against the crumbling mortar. He was more exhausted than he could ever remember and feeling the weight of his responsibility.

"Anything happening in front of us?" he shouted to a Sergeant peering through one of the ground floor windows.

"Nothing."

"Any word from the convoy?" his red-raw eyes searched until he found an RTO.

"ETA twenty minutes," she said. "A dozen Strykers and four Black Hawks are on their way."

Curry grunted. Twenty minutes...The Company's wounded were lined up against the south wall of the building because it was the most protected and because they could quickly be evacuated. Some of the men, he knew, would not survive the evacuation, despite the desperate efforts of the blood-spattered medics that hovered over them attentively.

With a tremendous effort of will, Curry forced himself to his feet. He tottered for a moment like a drunk, waves of vertiginous fatigue washing over him so that he was compelled to lunge for a handhold to keep himself upright. He went to the nearest window. Somewhere in the distance he could hear the faint beat of helicopter rotors.

To the north, the bomb-ruined debris of Kaesong seemed to stretch for miles. Here and there buildings still stood, but most structures had taken several hits, turning the vista into a grey bleak carnage. It reminded Curry of the path of destruction left by a tornado. Smoke blotted out much of the skyline, shrouding everything in a drifting haze.

Then a shot rang out.

It had come from somewhere ahead of him; from somewhere amidst the apocalyptic ruins. Then another mortar round arced through the air and exploded on the far side of the highway.

"Here they come!" someone at the far corner of the building shouted and the cry was echoed by several other men a split-second later. Curry dashed across the room and peered through the smoke. He could see hundreds of small dark shapes scattered in the ruins, dashing and darting towards their position in spasms of urgent movement.

The company's two HMGs were positioned on the third floor. Curry heard one of the heavy guns roar to life, chattering a thunder of death. The enemy returned fire. They had positioned machine guns in the rubble and in a building to the west. Suddenly the 'Culprits' were caught in a deadly crossfire as bullets seemed to whip and saw from every direction.

Curry threw himself to the ground. Bullets chewed the edges of the window and the air filled with concrete dust and flying shards. He heard a man grunt and then he saw a figure sag to his knees, clutching at his bloodied face.

"Fire!" Curry scrambled to his feet and raised his M4, thrusting the barrel through the mangled ruin of the window. A handful of dark darting figures were scrambling down a rubble strewn alley about three hundred yards to his north. He opened fire on the figures, saw one man go down hard, but lost sight of the others behind an explosion of white smoke.

Chapter 12:

"ETA five minutes!" the tension in Captain Grill's voice sounded clearly across the radio. The comms line between the convoy and 'Culprit' Company stayed hot and the RTO in a corner of the building could hear the commander of the Strykers swearing and exclaiming in the background as the vehicles came under attack. The Strykers were within the city limits now, still closing on the Company's location but taking hits from small arms fire.

Two Black Hawks peeled off the formation and flew on ahead, circling the target building. 'Culprit' Company were coming under heavy attack and the helicopters swooped low with their door gunners firing their M-240H machine guns into the advancing enemy. The added firepower was enough to stall the North Korean infantry. They had reached the surrounds of the building but now they fell back, like a receding wave being sucked back into the ocean. From somewhere amidst the rubble and RPG projectile streaked into the air, missing the nearest Black Hawk by a hundred yards but giving the crew onboard a heart-in-mouth moment of terror.

'Culprit' Company's RTO relayed the Stryker Company's ETA and Curry frowned, trying to sense the momentum of the firefight. It was going to be a near-run thing.

He circled the ground floor, offering words of encouragement to his men while they fired and the enemy shot back, the air fizzing with hot lead. At a window on the far side of the room where two rookie recruits fresh from the States were positioned, he slapped one of the soldiers on the back to get her attention. The woman's face was nicked and bleeding from concrete fragments.

"Get up to the third floor and let Sergeant Breevor know that the Stryker convoy will be here in five minutes. I want everyone from that floor down here in two minutes ready to evac. Understand?"

The soldier nodded, then darted towards the stairs, her body doubled-over as enemy bullets seemed to hunt her.

Curry took her place at the window and emptied his magazine into the distance. Targets were hard to find. The North Koreans were using the rubbled ruins well, firing from concealed heavy cover. Curry sensed the firefight was devolving into a stalemate. He could hear the Black Hawks circling overhead but out of his line of sight. The thump of their rotors came in thundering waves as they swooped and strafed the enemy. He saw the dark flitting shadow of one of the choppers leap and dance across the ground, the passage of the helicopter whipping up a dust storm of debris as it pirouetted in the air.

A grenade exploded against the northern façade of the building and Curry rolled his shoulder and flattened himself against the wall as a billow of smoke and a hail of fragments erupted through the window. Then, above the endless chatter of machine gun fire, he heard a chorus of strangled cries and realized the North Koreans were mounting a fresh wave of attacks. He jinked back in front of the window and fired into the smoke. For sixty furious seconds the North Koreans attacked, surging forward and taking heavy losses. The ground around the building's perimeter became littered with dead. Curry added to the death toll, emptying a second magazine into a tight knot of enemy soldiers from such close range that he could see the enemy soldier's faces clearly, their mouths open as they shouted their savage cry. One of Curry's bullets hit a man in the face, snapping his head back and punching him brutally to the ground, dead before his body hit the dirt. Two more bullets punched great bleeding holes in another enemy soldier's chest. His body seemed to disintegrate as he collapsed behind a red mist.

Once again, the North Koreans were repulsed. They retreated under a veil of smoke grenades, dragging their wounded with them and leaving trails of fresh blood. One man screamed in pain as two of his comrades carried him between them. Another man left behind in the aftermath of the assault clawed at the dirt, pulling himself remorselessly closer to the building, his jaw clenched. He had been struck by several bullets but was still alive. His legs were dead weights behind him as he dragged himself forward, his eyes blazing with fanaticism. He rolled onto his side and fumbled for a grenade. Sergeant Breevor tracked the man from a window on the third floor. As the North Korean reached back to toss the grenade at the building, Breevor shot him in the head, killing him. The grenade dropped from the lifeless hand and three seconds later exploded, heaving the North Korean's corpse several feet into the air and eviscerating the body into a bloody, steaming mush.

"Downstairs!" Breevor reeled away from the window and bellowed to the men around him. "We are evacuating!"

Then suddenly a fresh roar of noise challenged the clamor of combat. It was the sound of snarling diesel engines. Curry turned and peered. Through a shattered window he saw two Strykers race past the building and then suddenly swerve, forming a steel roadblock across the blacktop thirty yards further along the highway. The two Strykers parked broadside to shelter the infantry as they evacuated, their remote-control turrets turning and their snarling 50cal machine guns hunting danger. Ten seconds later a dark steel silhouette braked in front of the building's doors and Captain Gill stepped down onto the sidewalk.

He came swaggering in through the front doors, his face working with agitation and tension but his voice a fraud of calm composure that fooled no one.

"Someone called for a fleet of taxis?"

Curry peeled himself off the wall and the two men met in the middle of the rubble-strewn floor. Curry pointed to the North Korean prisoners. "Take them first, and then the wounded."

*

An RPG streaked through the air and struck one of the two Strykers that were formed up to barricade the highway and protect the troops in the building as they evacuated. The projectile struck the vehicle flush, destroying two of the ICV's huge tires and setting the rubber on fire. Thick black smoke from the explosion washed over the highway and the vehicle sagged at an angle. The driver evacuated but the vehicle commander stayed at his post, remotely firing the 50cal until the ammunition ran out.

When the commander finally evacuated the stricken Stryker and ran back to the shelter of the building, the North Korean prisoners and all of 'Culprit' Company's wounded had already been loaded aboard the trailing vehicles. The convoy was formed up and facing south, ready to exfil. Curry ordered the troops on the second floor to abandon their positions and make for the vehicles. Now there were just the survivors of 2nd Platoon defending the perimeter. Sergeant Breevor joined them as the rest of the Company crammed, sweaty and bleeding, into the waiting vehicles. Captain Gill ordered the surviving Stryker from the roadblock back to the front doors of the building. "We're out of here in two minutes," he shouted to Richard Curry above a sudden burst of 50cal fire from one of the Black Hawks circling overhead.

The Captain was peering through a ground floor window and could see dark vague silhouettes of the enemy in the far distance, massing for yet another attack. "Move your ass or get left behind."

It wasn't that simple and both men knew it. If the North Koreans surged forward, they could only be restrained with massed firepower. If Curry pulled his men away from the windows for loading aboard the Strykers, the North Koreans would overwhelm their position before the vehicles could make their escape.

"You do what you've gotta do," Curry said grimly. "Don't wait for us!"

Gill seemed torn between his need to evacuate the city and his obligation to Curry and the handful of men who stoically remained at their positions covering the exfiltration. He gave Curry a long hard look of grudging respect. "Where's your CO?"

"Dead."

"What about your XO?"

"Dead."

Gill grunted, then sighed. "Okay. You've got four minutes... but that's it. If you and the rest of your men aren't aboard a Stryker by then, you're on your own."

*

One of the men at a window, his head swathed in bloody bandages, began to sing *'America the Brave'*. It was bizarre, but in the madness of the moment and the sheer recklessness of their situation, others joined him in the patriotic act of defiance until every one of the remaining men was belting out the anthem at the top of their voices like an arrogant taunt to the enemy.

Curry tried to guess how much time had passed since Captain Gill had given his warning. He wondered how advanced the evacuation was, but he could not see the building's doors from where he stood, nor could he abandon his position at a window to go and look for himself. So instead, he checked his weapon was loaded with a fresh magazine and stared out through the window into the distance, praying the enemy would take just a few more precious minutes to organize themselves before they mounted their next attack. He could hear voices barking orders from the opposite side of the big room; everyone was infected with desperation and panic. In the back of his head his mind was counting down the seconds as he tried to judge the moment when he could finally shout the order to abandon the building.

"Start making for the convoy," he gave the order to a dozen men, releasing the soldiers in stages.

Then a bugle sounded from somewhere in the smoke-stained distance and everything went to hell.

The North Koreans charged.

"Fire!" Curry had held the best men in the Platoon to defend the walls while the rest began a frantic rush for the waiting Strykers. At his shoulder were Ethan Breevor and Buff Loftham, all of them shooting from the one broad window.

Curry reloaded his M4 and looked behind him. The evacuating soldiers were crammed into the doorway, waiting their turn to spill out onto the sidewalk and then into one of the waiting ICVs.

"Keep firing!"

An enemy bullet gouged shards of concrete from around the window sill and Ethan Breevor's brow was cut, strickling bright blood down his craggy face.

"Get out of here!" Curry seized the Sergeant by the shoulder and pushed him away from the window. "Get to the Strykers!"

The North Koreans were within a hundred yards of the northern wall. They were slowed by the mounds of dead bodies that acted like a breakwall, forcing them to scramble over their own dead and dying. A thrown grenade landed well short of the building and exploded. An enemy machine gun fired from the rubble, forcing two Americans at a nearby window to duck for frantic cover as a hail of bullets blasted holes in the wall on the far side of the room. The ground floor began to fill with smoke.

The enemy machine gun fire became so thundering that the defenders were forced to cringe into cover for several long seconds, allowing the North Korean infantry in the attack to scramble over the mounds of bodies and mount a final charge towards the building. The sound of their cries became exhilarated as they surged towards the northern wall.

Then Buff Loftham jinked into view with a SAW hanging from his hip.

Framed by the broken window and exposed to the enemy, Loftham roared a shout of savage defiance, clenched his jaw, and then opened fire.

He was a huge fearsome sight. His uniform was torn, his body drenched in blood and sweat and grime. He looked like some mythical monster risen from a gruesome legend. He triggered the M249 and the weapon began to spit death at seven hundred rounds per minute.

The range was so close and the enemy so densely packed as they compressed to attack the exposed windows that Loftham could not possibly miss. The light machine gun juddered in his hands, the recoil so unremarkable that he barely felt the kick through his body. The weapon's awesome firepower cut a swathe through the North Koreans who had no cover and no alternative other than to run onto the fire-spitting fury of the gun.

An enemy officer, driven on by his pride and his savage loathing of the Americans died in a gory explosion of torn flesh and blood. Three men running at his shoulder went down, as if falling in slow motion. They sagged to the ground clutching at gut and chest wounds, terrible agony in their faces but still screaming their blood-curdling cries of hatred.

Curry and the rest of the survivors added their own fire to the fury of the SAW. Ethan Breevor threw two grenades and then reluctantly made for the doorway, dragging a handful of other men with him. He called over his shoulder to Richard Curry, his hands cupped to his mouth to make himself heard.

"Get out now!" Breevor bellowed. "It's over. Get to the vehicles!"

Curry fired into the seething mass of North Koreans until his magazine clicked on an empty chamber. He thumped Buff Loftham on the helmet to get the giant man's attention. "We're going!"

The men who had remained at the windows suddenly abandoned their positions and rushed for the doorway. Close behind them and still swarming forward despite their appalling losses, the North Koreans launched a final charge.

There was nothing orderly about the scramble for the Strykers. There were just three vehicles with their rear ramps down, awaiting the last of the defenders. The vehicle's engines were revving wildly, the rest of the ICVs already in column formation and facing south. Curry waited at the door until the last of his men was on the sidewalk and then he lobbed two smoke grenades into the empty room in the hope it would buy the few precious seconds his men needed to reach safety.

The North Koreans reached the ground floor windows and a handful of grenades rattled across the broken floorboards. They exploded in a deafening series of thunderous roars. Flames stabbed through the black smoke and a flail of shrapnel blasted around the room. Curry felt something searingly hot tug at his left forearm and then a wash of blood spilled over his sleeve.

He burst through the door and into the smoke hazed daylight. His wounded arm felt like it was on fire. He could see the rear ramps of the two closest Strykers rising and he ran past them, his legs heavy with exhaustion and sweat streaming into his eyes. When he reached the lowered ramp of the last waiting vehicle, a huge hand seemed to pull him off his feet. "Move your ass!" Buff Loftham had no time for formality or respect for rank.

The burly Corporal heaved Curry into the gloomy cramped interior and then pounded his palm against the inside wall of the Stryker as a signal to the anxious driver. The ramp began to rise and even before it was up, the vehicle was moving, its engine howling and its turret turning as the onboard 50cal fired to cover their retreat.

Curry rolled onto his side and spat a mouthful of blood. The steel interior was crammed with a jumble of gasping, bleeding men. A sudden explosion rocked the vehicle, and for a moment it seemed to teeter on the verge of tipping over. Then the Stryker righted itself again, the engine still revving but the vehicle responding sluggishly. The men crammed into the hull of the Stryker were thrown around like tenpins as the ICV seemed to veer out of control. Curry's head cracked against the steel floor.

Outside the vehicle a series of nearby explosions rocked the Stryker on its suspension and rattled the interior with a hail of shrapnel hits. The vehicle took a direct hit from an RPG. The shattering impact of the blast against the steel cage armor was enough to heave the rear of the Stryker off its wheels. The interior filled with swirling smoke and dust. Men began to choke. Someone screamed in panic and confusion. Curry could hear the vehicle's commander and the driver shouting, but he could make no sense of the words.

Another explosion rocked the ICV and then the roar of enemy fire seemed to fade. Curry clung to the vehicle's steel bench as the Stryker swerved suddenly, then surged forward. Someone in the press of bodies let out a long gasp of relief and then cheered.

Curry got to his feet and prised open one of the rear hatches. A rush of fresh air filed the interior. He peered into the haze. He could see the building wreathed in smoke and he could see another Stryker following close behind them as the outskirts of Kaesong city slid away into the smoky distance.

The fight was over. They had escaped.

Epilogue:

Two days after 'Culprit' Company's escape, Kaesong city fell to the Americans. In the aftermath of the triumph Richard Curry was summonsed to Colonel Gallman's tent. The order was delivered by a Battalion aide who escorted the Lieutenant. Curry followed like a man due for the executioner's axe. The survivors from 'Culprit' Company saw their Lieutenant being escorted away and they rose to their feet and rendered Curry a solemn but heartfelt salute.

Everyone knew he was facing a court-martial.

Ethan Breevor shook Curry's hand. Curry felt himself flush with awkward embarrassment. He was completely unprepared for the outpouring of support and emotion from the battle-hardened Company. He walked with his back straight because all he had left was his pride.

Lieutenant Colonel Gallman was waiting behind his desk when Curry entered the tent. Gallman made the rookie officer wait until he read through a report and signed the document with a flourish. He turned cold steely eyes on Curry and the resentment seethed from him.

"You smart-ass son-of-a-bitch," Gallman spoke quietly, as though he did not want this exchange overheard. "Who the fuck do you think you are, Curry, telling me to go and fuck myself when I gave you a direct order? *Who the fuck do you think you are?*"

Curry said nothing. He stood rigidly at attention and fixed his gaze on a tear in the tent's canvas a few inches above Gallman's head. He remained unblinking while the Lieutenant Colonel's temper burst like a thunderstorm around him.

"I gave you a choice, you jumped-up little bastard! I said you could follow my leadership example, or follow Captain fucking Hector – and you chose Hector! Do you think you're immune from authority? Do you think you won't be held accountable for disobeying my orders?"

Curry flinched. He had expected this torrent of abuse but even he was shocked by the outpouring of vile hatred Gallman spewed. It was like standing in the eye of a hurricane as the accusations slashed and whipped about him.

Then suddenly the tent's flaps twitched aside and General Barett strode into the tent. Gallman choked on his words and flushed crimson with embarrassment. He wondered guiltily how much the General had overhead before he had revealed himself. Barett smiled warmly.

"Colonel Gallman, please forgive my interruption – but I couldn't miss the opportunity to meet the Hero of Kaesong city personally." Barrett clapped Richard Curry on the shoulder. "Son, that North Korean officer your boys captured was a Field Marshall. Did you know that?"

"No sir," Curry was numb with shock.

"Well, that sonofabitch was responsible for the defense of the city – and you caught him. The intelligence we learned from interrogating the guy was directly attributable to the success of our subsequent attack. In short, we won the Battle for Kaesong because of your actions. Thousands of men are alive today because of you. It was an example of outstanding initiative and inspirational leadership," the General heaped praise on Curry and then turned to include Gallman in his comments.

"I'm sure your Battalion commander is just as proud of you as the rest of the Army is, right Colonel?"

Gallman flushed indignantly. "Yes, sir," the words were like broken glass in his mouth. "Of course."

"Good!" General Barret said and gave Gallman a pointed glare of warning. "Because I think this young firebrand of an officer is in line for a battlefield commission. Would a promotion to Captain have your support, Colonel?"

Gallman had been railroaded into a corner. He nodded his head, signalling his agreement, and his abdication. Richard Curry had survived a second attack in less than two days, managing to keep the Company intact and now his career too.

When Curry strode from the Colonel's tent, the 'Culprits' were standing in the mud waiting for him.

"No court-martial?" Ethan Breevor's smile showed his relief.

"No."

"So, what happens next?"

Curry shrugged. "I guess we march with the Army north towards Pyongyang."

"For another fight?"

"Yes. For another fight."

Because the Battle for Kaesong was over.

Links to other titles in the collection:
- **Charge to Battle**
- **Enemy in Sight**
- **Viper Mission**
- **Fort Suicide**
- **The Killing Ground**
- **Search and Destroy**
- **Airborne Assault**
- **Defiant to the Death**
- **A Time for Heroes**

Facebook: https://www.facebook.com/NickRyanWW3
Website: https://www.worldwar3timeline.com

Acknowledgements:

The greatest thrill of writing, for me, is the opportunity to research the subject matter and to work with military, political and historical experts from around the world. I had a lot of help researching this book from the following groups and people. I am forever grateful for their willing enthusiasm and cooperation. Any remaining technical errors are mine.

Jill Blasy:

Jill has the editorial eye of an eagle! I trust Jill to read every manuscript, picking up typographical errors, missing commas, and for her general 'sense' of the book. Jill has been a great friend and a valuable part of my team for several years.

Jan Wade:

Jan is my Personal Assistant and an indispensable part of my team. She is a thoughtful, thorough, professional and persistent pleasure to work with. Chances are, if you're reading this book, it's due to Jan's engaging marketing and promotional efforts.

Dale Simpson:

Dale is a retired Special Forces operator who has been helping me with the military aspects of my writing since I first put pen to paper. He is my first point of contact for military technical advice. Over the years that he has been saving me from stupid mistakes we've become firm friends. The authenticity of the action and combat sequences in this novel are due to Dale's diligence and willing cooperation.

Dion Walker Sr:

Sergeant First Class (Retired) Dion Walker Sr, served 21 proud years in the US Army with deployments during Operation Desert Shield/Storm, Operation Intrinsic Action and Operation Iraqi Freedom. For 17 years he was a tanker in several Armor Battalions and Cavalry Squadrons before spending 4 years as an MGS (Stryker Mobile Gun System) Platoon Sergeant in a Stryker Infantry Company.

Kwuantae Santana-Rice:

Staff Sergeant Kwuantae 'Pedro' Santana-Rice spent four years in the Marines on the M198 and the M777 howitzer, and twelve years in the North Carolina National Guard on the M109A6/A7 self-propelled howitzer. He has deployed five times to war zones, including during Operation Iraqi Freedom, twice for Operation Inherent Resolve and twice during Operation Enduring Freedom. He is currently an active-service member of the Armed Forces.

Printed in Great Britain
by Amazon